I looked up from the script. Smiling encouragement from the fourth row was Todd Bowers. Why was he here this afternoon? Had he come just to see me?

. . . I don't know precisely when I lost my balance. I only remember the sickening sensation of tilting forward, grappling with empty air, and meeting the floor in a tangle of flailing arms and legs. There were gasps of horror, someone shrieked, and then voices shouted back and forth all around me. I gazed up at a ring of frightened faces.

"I'm all right," I said. "Don't worry about me! I'm fine!"

I wasn't fooling anybody. My shoulder throbbed. Something had happened to my right shin and my left ankle. I struggled to sit up.

The crowd parted to let Mom through. I wondered dimly where she had been waiting. Had she seen me try out? Or had she only seen me fall?

Todd saw me fall, too. He saw my mother rushing to collect me. He heard the shouts, and saw me splayed out on the floor.

This was, without a doubt, the worst moment of my entire life.

"Chloe!" Mom cried, and her face was white. "What happened? What's wrong? Chloe!"

Why Me?

THE COURAGE TO LIVE

DEBORAH KENT

AN ARCHWAY PAPERBACK
Published by POCKET BOOKS
New York London Toronto Sydney Singapore

AN ARCHWAY PAPERBACK *Original*

An Archway Paperback published by
POCKET BOOKS, a division of Simon & Schuster, Inc.
1230 Avenue of the Americas, New York, NY 10020

Copyright © 2001 by Deborah Kent

ISBN: 0-7434-0031-3

First Archway Paperback printing February 2001

10 9 8 7 6 5 4 3 2 1

AN ARCHWAY PAPERBACK and colophon are
registered trademarks of Simon & Schuster, Inc.

Front cover illustration by Sandy Young/Studio Y

Printed in the U.S.A.

IL 6+

To Dick and Janna,
my inspiration, my support,
my foundation

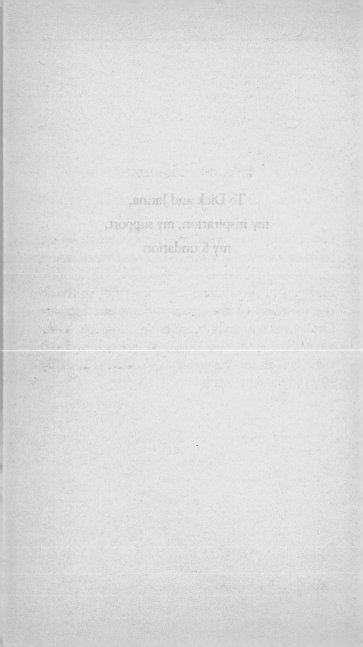

To Dick and Janna,
my inspiration, my support,
my foundation

Acknowledgments

I would like to extend my deepest appreciation to Mary Pat Scotkovsky of the Lupus Foundation of America, Illinois Chapter, for her careful reading of this manuscript. I also wish to thank the members of the Lupus Adolescent Support Group at La Rabida Hospital in Chicago. They were eager to discuss this book project, and did their best to set me straight on what it is really like to live with lupus.

Why Me?

THE COURAGE TO LIVE

1

"She never did," I said. "Megan McAllister never turned in her raffle money."

Samantha's groan felt like a hammer blow to my skull. I winced and held the phone at arm's length.

"She *never* remembers *anything*! I told her Thursday! I told her yesterday! I told her—"

Samantha was winding up to a full-blown rant as the front door banged open, pounding my head with yet another shock wave. Dad gestured frantically from the porch. "Chloe, aren't you ready yet?" he demanded. "I've been waiting out in the car for the past five minutes!"

"Just a second, Sam," I said, though she probably didn't hear me. I cupped my hand over the mouthpiece and told Dad, "I've got to straighten out this one last thing."

"I have six errands to run," he fumed. "If you want a ride, now's the time!" The door banged again, and he was gone.

I went back to Samantha. "Listen," I said, "I've got to go to work. Call Megan and remind her to—"

"I bet she forgot where she put the envelope. She probably forgot we need it by Monday. That girl could forget her own name!"

"I have to go!" I pleaded. "Just call her, okay?"

"It'll be a waste of time. She is totally unto-gether! She—"

My head pounded unbearably. I felt im-mensely tired.

"Okay, don't call her then," I said. "What-ever."

"I'm sorry," Samantha said quickly. "I didn't mean to give you a hard time. I'll take care of it somehow."

Dad leaned on the horn as I thanked her and said good-bye. I grabbed my jacket and stood up, but my head gave such a thump I almost had to sit down again. As I lurched to the front door, I nearly tripped over our black kitten, Trixie.

Trina, the white kitten, watched from the back of the couch. She almost seemed to be laughing.

"Coming!" I called, catching hold of a chair to keep my balance. The phone started ringing again. It was probably for me. It might even be Megan, with the whereabouts of the Drama Club raffle money. I thought of turning back to pick it up. But no—I was due at The Shelter in three minutes, and it was a ten-minute drive.

"Well!" Dad said as I climbed into the front seat. "How many hats are you wearing today?"

I didn't feel like being teased. Besides, the thought of wearing even one hat made my head throb more than ever. "I'm going to be late," I said. "Dr. Pat will kill me."

Dad flashed a wicked grin. "Dr. Pat won't kill you. She'll just put you to sleep!"

I searched fruitlessly for a good comeback as we merged onto the expressway. My mind had gone blank. I sat in silence, pressing my hand to my forehead, until Dad pulled up in front of the animal shelter where I worked every Saturday.

My legs felt stiff as I stepped down to the pavement. The world revolved slowly before my eyes, and I gripped the door handle for support.

"You okay?" Dad asked, concerned.

I nodded. Lately, people asked me that question all the time. I was tired so much it made me light-headed. I had too much to do, that was the trouble. Maybe Mom was right, and I ought to drop French Club, or twirling, or something. Maybe I should just drop school! Now, there was a thought! I could sleep in every morning, and never have to worry about papers or exams. I'd have six extra hours, five days a week! It sounded glorious!

Buoyed by that cheery thought, I walked through the door with a smile. A chorus of barks erupted from the kennel in back, the way it always did when a new human arrived. Dr. Pat sat at the desk, talking to a gray-haired woman who held a cat carrier. "Chloe! Thank goodness you're here!" she exclaimed. "The place is jumping!"

I had worked at The Shelter for the past two years, ever since I was a freshman. I was a natural, I suppose. When I was little, I was always bringing home stray cats and dogs, or rescuing baby birds that had fallen out of the nest. If anyone asked what I wanted to be when I grew up, I said, "An animal doctor." I got the job at The Shelter through Dr. Pat—her name was really Dr. Patriciano, but she was Dr. Pat to everyone.

Dr. Pat was an old friend of Mom's from college. She was a veterinarian, with her own practice on weekdays. On Saturdays she put in time at The Shelter, taking care of animals that were lost or homeless. The Shelter was short-staffed on weekends, and Dr. Pat always had plenty of work to keep me busy.

Now she pointed to the cat carrier, which the gray-haired woman set on the counter. "This guy's going to need the whole workup," Dr. Pat told me. "Take him in back, okay?"

I peered into the box, expecting to see a glaring feline. Instead, I discovered a brown and white puppy huddled in a corner. It had thick, drooping ears like a cocker spaniel.

"Oh! It's a dog!" I exclaimed. "He's so cute!"

The gray-haired woman watched wistfully. "I wish I could keep him myself," she said. "Somebody will want him, don't you think?"

"Sure," I agreed. "Puppies are easy."

I carried the puppy in its box to one of the examining rooms. From here the din was almost deafening—yaps, howls, and now and then a big bass woof. From across the hall floated the plaintive mews and wails of The Shelter's cat population. I rubbed my throbbing head and wished I could lie down, just for a few minutes. Just to rest.

Well, rest wasn't an option. I opened the box and reached in, holding my hand still so the puppy could sniff my fingers. "See, it's okay," I told him. "You won't like getting your shots, though. It's a good thing you don't know what I'm talking about." He didn't understand the words, but he seemed to like the sound of my voice. He wriggled and wagged and licked my hand.

"How're we doing back here?" asked Dr. Pat as she breezed in. She scooped the puppy from the box and set him gently on the table. I watched as she examined him from nose to tail—peering into his eyes, ears, and mouth, running expert hands over his squirming body.

"Looks healthy to me," she said. "Hold him a second; he'd like to make a break for it!"

I held the puppy by the scruff of his neck while Dr. Pat got ready. Every animal dropped off at The Shelter had to get shots against things like rabies and distemper. In addition, each one had to go through ten days of quarantine before it could be adopted.

Dr. Pat talked as she worked. "I need you to give some baths. That big Lab—he's a sweet guy, he won't give you a hard time. Then there's that feisty little mutt—you know, the beagle cross. Think you can handle her?"

"Sure," I said. I knew the dog she meant. She was a real escape artist. She'd try to bolt whenever you opened her cage.

"Okay," said Dr. Pat. "Go ahead and get started."

She put the puppy back into his box and headed toward the quarantine wing. "Did he get his shots already?" I asked. "I didn't even notice."

"All done," she assured me. "What a good boy! Not a yip out of him!"

"I think it's the way you do it," I told her. "They all like you."

"It's just experience," she said. "You get the hang of it if you do it a lot."

I went out to the bathing room and ran a couple of inches of lukewarm water into the stainless-steel tub. Then I opened the door to the kennel.

The barking engulfed me. Up and down the rows of cages, every dog shouted for attention. Most Saturdays I walked from one to the next, getting reacquainted with old friends and saying hello to new arrivals. But today I went straight to the glossy black Labrador in his cage on the end. "Hey there, Mike!" I said, unfastening the door. "You having a good day?"

Dr. Pat had warned me not to give names to any of the animals at The Shelter. If I named them, I was more likely to get attached to them, and feel sad when they were given away, or if they had to be put to sleep. I tried to "stay objective," as she suggested. But sometimes I couldn't help myself. The Lab, with his quiet alertness, was an individual. I couldn't resist giving him a name of his own.

I clipped a leash to Mike's collar and led him to his fate. He walked sedately beside me, not protesting, but showing no trace of excitement either. When we entered the bathing room, he cowered for a moment, hunching against the floor. Then he seemed to gather his courage. He gave me a beseeching look, straightened up, and let me boost him into the tub.

Mike was the most easygoing dog I'd ever seen—a real gentleman, Dr. Pat called him. But we'd had him almost a month, and no one had adopted him. The Shelter was only allowed to keep animals for ninety days. I tried not to think about what would happen if Mike didn't find an owner in the next two months.

I finished with Mike in ten minutes, and rubbed him dry with one of the rough dog towels we used. He looked fantastic, all sleek and shining. The next time someone walked in to adopt a dog, I hoped they would find him irresistible.

As soon as Mike was in his cage again, I went to look at the beagle cross, the dog Dr. Pat called the "feisty little mutt." I called her Pins-and-Needles, Pins for short. Pins was never still. She bounced from one wall of her cage to the other, or pawed frantically at the door. Now, as I approached, she exploded into barking and wagging, quivering from nose to tail. It made me tired just to watch her. I couldn't imagine how it would feel to have so much energy!

Better get it over with, I told myself. *Once she's finished you can sit down and rest.*

Slowly, carefully, I slid open the cage door. Pins was right there, waiting for a chance to slip out. I snapped a leash onto her collar and wound it around my hand for good measure. Just to be on the safe side, I even slipped a light leather muzzle over her jaws. Dr. Pat had taught me that it paid to be cautious.

"Okay, girl, come on out," I said. Pins burst forth like a ball from a cannon. She gave such a tug on the leash that she almost jerked me off my feet.

"Stop it!" I cried. "Calm down!" I tried to jerk back on the leash, the way Dr. Pat had taught me, but somehow my arm wasn't strong enough. For a few moments Pins and I were locked in a tug-of-war. Finally, coaxing and hauling, I got her into the bathing room. Luckily, she wasn't very big—only about twenty pounds—so I managed to hoist her up and over the rim of the tub. For an instant she stood stock-still in the water, frozen with amazement. Then she gave a tremendous bound, the leash whirled out of my grasp, and Pins vanished through the open door.

"Hey!" I yelled, lunging after her. In the hall I grabbed uselessly for the trailing leash, but Pins whisked it beyond my reach.

She paused in the doorway and gave a mighty shake, splattering drops of water everywhere. Then she raced into the front office and leaped up on Dr. Pat, who sat at the desk with the phone in her hand.

Dr. Pat gave a little shriek of surprise and grabbed for Pins' leash, but the dog evaded her, too. The leash snagged around the leg of a chair.

Pins gave another bound, the chair overturned, and she was free again.

At that precise moment the door opened. Two boys stepped inside, one tiny and the other tall. Pins hurled herself at their legs.

In one smooth, swift gesture, the tall boy dipped and straightened again, holding Pins' leash aloft.

"Whew!" he said, laughing. "The catch of the day!"

Pins crouched at his feet, trembling with the excitement of the chase. She knew it was over, but I had the feeling she had loved every moment.

Slowly, my mind took in the people before me. The smaller boy was seven or eight, his grin showing the gap of missing front teeth. The other boy was tall and blond, and familiar in his Woodstock High School sweatshirt. I'd seen those laughing blue eyes before.

"Aren't you Todd Bowers?" I asked.

"Yeah," he said. He eyed me closely. "You're in fifth lunch, right? I see you with Sam Ryles."

"Right. I knew I'd seen you around."

"Is this the dog we're taking home?" the little boy piped up.

Todd looked down. "I don't know," he said.

"We've got to look around first." He turned back to me. "It's Ian's birthday," he explained. "Mom promised he could get a puppy—he's wanted one forever."

By now Dr. Pat was off the phone. She took charge of Pins, and sent me to introduce Todd and Ian to the puppies that were up for adoption. We had six at the moment—four from a litter of shepherd-collie crosses, a dachshund, and a very cute part-golden retriever.

Ian fell in love with the golden at first sight. "I think her name is Mocha," he said, cuddling her in his arms.

"Mocha?" I asked. "How come?"

Ian looked blank. "It just is," was all he could tell me.

"He's like that," Todd said over Ian's head. "He gets these ideas, and you can't change his mind."

I nodded. A wave of weakness swept over me, weighing down my whole body. Chasing Pins had robbed me of my last bit of strength. I forced my legs to carry me to the front office, where I handed Todd the adoption papers and the forms about bringing Mocha back for booster shots and neutering. I heard myself giving explanations, answering questions, but the voice belonged to someone else, far away. I had only one clear thought—I had to sit down. My legs folded beneath me and I sagged into a chair. Across the distance, Todd's voice asked the familiar question, "Are you okay?"

"I guess . . . not."

Dr. Pat came in and placed a cool hand on my forehead. "You feel a little feverish," she said. "Maybe you'd better go home early."

"Mom can't pick me up till four-thirty," I said bleakly. I wanted only to crawl into bed. And that was impossible. Impossible.

"I can give you a ride home," Todd volunteered. He looked away shyly and added, "If that's okay."

Somehow my tired brain took in the weirdness of the situation. Todd was totally cute. I had always admired him from a distance. I couldn't connect him with one particular crowd at school; I'd seen him with football players and nerds and everybody in between. He was the kind of guy who seemed to like everyone—and everyone liked him, too. Now here he was, Todd Bowers himself, at The Shelter with his little brother! Todd Bowers was offering me a ride! And I was too sick even to be thrilled.

He wasn't offering because he liked me, I reminded myself. I had nearly fainted dead away, like the heroine of some old-fashioned novel. Todd was a nice guy, ready to lend a helping hand. He wanted to help me out, like a Boy Scout guiding an old lady across the street.

"Well?" Todd asked. "You want a ride?"

"Sure," I murmured. "Thanks."

How would I face Todd on Monday in the caf? I'd cringe with embarrassment! But I couldn't think about the long-term future. I wanted only one thing right now—to get home. Ways and means didn't matter.

Todd and I had little to say on the ride to my house. Ian filled up the silence, chattering about Mocha, gleefully describing every wag of her tail and flick of her tongue. When Todd pulled up at our front walk, I thanked him again and climbed out.

"You want me to walk you to the door?" he asked, his voice worried.

I shook my head; it took too much effort to speak. I needed every ounce of energy for the trip along the sidewalk, up the steps, to the front door. One . . . two . . . three . . . four steps—and my key turned in the lock. I looked back at

Todd, watching me anxiously from the driver's seat. I waved, and he waved back before his car pulled away.

As I crossed the living room, I heard voices in the kitchen, low and serious. Mom and Dad sat at the table. My older sister, Caitlyn, stood by the sink, hands loose and empty at her sides. No one commented on my unexpected appearance. They were absorbed in something else.

"Hey," I said. "What's going on?"

Finally Mom looked my way. "Your father just heard some bad news."

Bad news? My brain fogged over. What could be worse than this—my aching stiffness, my pounding head, my longing to lie down and close out the light and noise of the world?

"Bad news," echoed Dad. "They're downsizing my department at work. Looks like I'm going to be out of a job."

2

On Monday I didn't go to school. My head
still ached, and I felt bone-weary even after ten
hours of sleep. When I took my temperature, it
was 100.8—not really much of a fever, but
enough to persuade Mom that I was sick.

"Looks like you're having a relapse," she said,
shaking her head. "When did you get over that
strep, anyway?"

"Three weeks ago," I said. "Remember, I was
too sick to go to that show with the Drama Club?"

"Stay home and catch up on your sleep," Mom
said. "You'll feel better tomorrow."

I knew the next day should show an improvement, but Tuesday morning I felt as bad as
I had the day before. Catching up on sleep

didn't seem to help. My hands felt stiff, and my knees complained bitterly as I staggered out of bed to the bathroom. My temperature was still a degree above normal. Maybe this *was* normal, I thought grimly. Maybe I had some kind of superflu, and I would be stuck feeling this way from now on.

I couldn't lie in bed for the rest of my life. Staying home didn't help me feel any better. I might as well go to school.

Mom barely glanced my way when I walked into the kitchen. She looked pale and tired herself, as though she hadn't slept in a week. I wondered if she was getting the same bug I had.

More likely she was worried about Dad's job. As I had lain in bed the night before, their voices had drifted up from the living room through the heating vents. I couldn't pick out words, but I heard the tones—a long, troubled murmur, rising every so often to a peak, and subsiding into the troubled depths once more. On most mornings, Dad was at the breakfast table, paging through the *Tribune*. Today, his chair stood empty. I asked Mom where he was.

"He went in early," Mom said. "He and some

of the people in his department are meeting to compare rumors."

"If it's only rumors, why worry?" asked Caitlyn from the doorway.

"Some rumors are based on facts," Mom said. She went to the sink and retreated behind a clatter of dishes. I could tell she didn't want to say more. When she wasn't looking, I gulped a couple of Tylenols with my orange juice.

I didn't think Caitlyn would notice either, but she stopped slicing her banana and gave me a long look. I headed her off before she could ask. "Yes," I said. "I'm okay! I'm fine!" But I knew deep down that it wasn't true.

The thought of Todd Bowers jarred me as I clambered down from the bus in front of the school. What would I say if I ran into him? I couldn't have looked more uncool last Saturday! First, I had displayed myself chasing a sopping dog around the office. And if that weren't bad enough, I had nearly collapsed with the super-bug! I might still have salvaged the day by coming to life on the ride home. But I hadn't thought of one worthwhile thing to say. I'd be just as tongue-tied if he spoke to me now. Not that he would, after Saturday's performance. How could I ever live it down?

Somehow I dragged myself through my morning classes. During English Lit, Mrs. Brinkerman sent us to the Learning Center to look up Elizabethan drama. I found a table at the back, put my head down, and slid into a fitful doze until the bell rang. I thought of staying there straight through lunch—food was the last thing on my mind! But I knew I should find Samantha, or Megan McAllister, or both of them. I ought to make sure the money from the Drama Club raffle was safe.

Samantha called to me as I emerged from the lunch line. I carried my tray to the table where she sat with Carrie Chang and Joni Schubert. "Is that all you're eating?" Joni asked, pointing to my container of salad.

"That's plenty," I said. "I'm not very hungry."

"It's not fair," said Carrie. "You skinny people always like skinny food, and the rest of us like brownies."

"Whenever I see somebody who looks like you, I get jealous," Joni said. She laughed without really smiling.

Carrie popped a handful of fries into her

mouth. "They ought to pass a dress code against thinness," she said, munching.

Even Sam got into the spirit. "Why not?" she said. "They have rules against everything else. No midriff shirts, no halter tops, no tight pants, no loose pants . . ."

"No weight below one-twenty allowed," Joni said. "Let's ban skinny people forever."

"You're not exactly fat, Joni," I protested. "I don't know what you're worried about."

"Ever notice how skinny people always say things like that?" Joni remarked to the others. "Big of them, isn't it?"

Her words stung. I wasn't trying to put anyone down. I'd been slender all my life—"the model type," people often told me. But Joni was lovely herself, with her delicate, round face, long eyelashes, and streaming blond hair. She had no reason to be jealous.

It was time to change the subject. "Did you call Megan?" I asked Sam.

She made a face. "She said she'd give me the money in homeroom. Guess what?"

"She forgot to bring it."

"How'd you know?"

"I must be psychic," I said.

Carrie and Joni giggled, but Sam was outraged. "Chloe, don't you even care?" she cried. "It's two hundred dollars! The money for the *Pygmalion* sets."

"I know. I can't think about it right now."

Samantha had a wonderful way of shifting gears. She pushed Drama Club aside and gave me her full attention. "What's wrong?" she asked. "Something's bothering you, huh?"

"I don't feel well," I muttered. I didn't want to go into details, especially with Joni and Carrie listening in.

"Go to the nurse," Carrie advised. "Maybe she'll send you home."

"Good old Mrs. Smalley," Joni snickered. "She offered me a Band-Aid when I went in with cramps the other day."

Sam refused to be sidetracked. "No, really," she said. "We can go right now. I'll walk down with you."

I shook my head. "It's not that kind of sick. I've been like this ever since—" How long had it been since I was full of energy, free from aches and pains? I'd never completely recovered from the strep throat I'd had back in January.

Samantha frowned. "Like, what's the matter, exactly?"

"I don't have any pep. I get these awful headaches. And I feel like an old grandma—all stiff and creaky."

"Maybe you'd better tell your mother," Sam said, "if you've had it for a long time."

"I did tell her," I said quickly. "She let me stay home yesterday." I dipped into my salad. It was limp and tasteless.

"Skip Mrs. Smalley," Carrie said. "Go to the doctor. Get on antibiotics."

"You think so?"

"Sure. They'll give you penicillin. Fix you right up."

"I was on antibiotics before. Ten days' worth."

"You need another ten days then," Sam said. "Don't suffer in silence."

Maybe she was right, I thought, with a surge of hope. The pills I took in January did help for a while. Maybe I needed another supply. I'd feel better right away. The very idea gave me a jolt of new life. I finished my salad and went back to the line for more to eat.

I was at the register, wallet in hand, when I looked over my shoulder. Standing in line, just two people behind me, was Todd Bowers.

My heart lurched. I wanted to look away, to pretend I hadn't seen him. But already it was too late. Todd's eyes locked on mine. "Hi, Chloe," he said. "How's it going?"

"Okay, I guess." *Oh, that was clever,* I scolded myself. *What a memorable comeback! Just the thing to snag his attention!*

Todd turned away. He was standing with two other guys, both of them on the soccer team. My hands shook as I counted my change. I glanced back at Todd. He and his friends were in a huddle, laughing about something, oblivious to me.

I made my way back to the table and settled down once more. "That's better," Joni said as I unwrapped a tuna sandwich. "Real mayonnaise. Put some pounds on you."

"Thanks a lot," I said. Already that surge of appetite was fading. I forced myself to eat—chew, swallow, chew, swallow—bite after uninspiring bite. The others chattered about a trip to the mall. I didn't comment. I didn't have the energy to eat and talk at the same time.

I was wadding up my empty wrapper when a male voice said, "Hi again!" Todd Bowers breezed past, heading to the rack with his empty tray.

"Hi!" I called after him. He didn't stop, but he waved my way with his free hand.

"Do you know him?" Samantha asked.

"I don't think so," I said. "But that's the second time this lunch he said hi to me."

"Well, well!" Joni said with a smirk. "Are you moving up in the world or what?"

"He said hi. That doesn't mean much." It didn't, I warned myself. He was only being polite, after Saturday. I was no one special to him. Somehow that thought filled me with an aching regret, beyond the dull, steady pounding in my head.

On Tuesday nights Mom went to her computer class right after work, and we usually had Chinese takeout. But today I came home to find Mom reading a magazine on the living room sofa. I knew this wasn't a normal day. "Hi, Chloe," she said, looking up distractedly. "There's a casserole in the fridge. You girls can heat it up."

"How come you're home?" I asked. "Didn't you go to work?"

"I came home early."

"You're going to eat out?" I felt like I had to drag the answers from her, one by one.

"Your father and I are going to Rizzuto's."

"Why? You never eat out on a weeknight." Maybe they had something to celebrate. Maybe Dad wasn't losing his job after all! But one look at Mom's face told me this wasn't a celebration dinner.

"We need to talk," she said. "We'll have to make some changes."

"Is it true, then? Dad's getting laid off?"

" 'Getting'?" Mom asked in a stunned voice. "It's done. Finished. They called him in today and sent him home."

"What?" I exclaimed. "Don't they have to give him a couple of weeks' notice? Don't they—"

"Not these days," Mom said bitterly. "They wouldn't even let him go back to his office alone. Security stood over him while he emptied his desk!"

I sank into a chair. It didn't make sense. It couldn't be true.

"Why?" I demanded. "Why would they do that? To Dad?"

"They did it to everybody," Mom assured me. "They're afraid people will sabotage the computers or something."

For fifteen years Dad had worked in public relations at Marlowe and Thurston. He'd been there almost my whole life. Once he had explained to me that his job was "persuading people that everything's all right, even if everything's all wrong." He joked about it, but I knew he loved working there. M & T was like a family, he always told us. The company couldn't have had a more loyal employee.

"Of six people in PR, they laid off four," Mom said. "Everybody's in shock."

"Where is he now?" I asked. "I didn't see the car."

"The company referred him to a job placement service. He went to see them."

"Well, then, he'll find something pretty soon," I said. It felt weird, to be reassuring my own mother this way.

"It won't be easy," Mom sighed. "I just don't think so."

"We can stay in Woodstock, right?" I asked anxiously. "We won't have to move!"

"If we're lucky," Mom said. "The whole Chicago area's tight right now. We might even have to go out of state."

For a few moments we were both silent. I tried not to think about what she'd said. Move away from all my friends, away from the neighborhood that had been home all my life? It was impossible! I wouldn't think of it. I couldn't.

"So, how was your day?" Mom asked after a while. "You have a lot of homework?"

"Not too much. Just finish my Shakespeare paper."

"You look better, that's for sure," Mom said. "I guess it's a good thing you stayed out yesterday."

"I'm still tired," I began. "I'm still not feeling all that good."

"Get to bed early," she said. "You get run-down when you don't sleep enough."

Sleep doesn't help, I wanted to tell her. *I wake up tired, as if I'd never been to bed.*

I needed a visit to Dr. Stanley, a prescription from the drugstore, and I would be myself again. Now was the time to explain, to get the process underway. "Mom," I began.

"What?" Her voice held a note of impatience. She had enough on her mind already.

I tried again. "Mom, I think I'm not really better. I—"

The front door opened before I could finish the sentence. Dad came in, his steps slow, his shoulders sagging. I'd never seen him look so old.

Mom sprang up to greet him. "How'd it go?" she asked, giving him a hug.

"I filled out a bunch of forms," Dad muttered. "They want me to take some tests, go to a workshop."

"And then?" Mom asked.

Dad shook his head. "They don't have anything for me," he said flatly. "It's all talk."

"We can't just sit back and wait!" Mom exclaimed.

"I'll keep looking," Dad promised. "But it's going to be a long haul."

They drifted into talk of severance packages and health insurance plans. I went quietly up to my room. This was no time to bring up my worries. I could wait till tomorrow.

Maybe one more good night's sleep *would* do the trick. Maybe I'd wake up refreshed, and I wouldn't need to see Dr. Stanley at all. Tomorrow was another day.

3

As soon as I woke the next morning, I knew that today was different. I stretched luxuriously, free from pain from head to toe. Bouncing out of bed, I sprinted for the bathroom, getting there inches ahead of Caitlyn. I even stepped aside to let her use it first. I was in such a good mood, it was fun to do her a favor.

I floated downstairs and found Dad at the breakfast table, poring over the classified ads. "Hi!" I said brightly, popping some bread into the toaster. "Mind if I put some music on?"

Dad looked up, frowning. "Please, not now!" he said. "I need to concentrate."

Usually Dad was a morning person, obnoxiously cheerful when I was only half-awake.

Now his tone had a sharp edge that made me wince. I didn't say another word. I made as little noise as I could while preparing breakfast.

I felt much better physically, but life on the home front took a downturn as the days wore on.

Dad was home when I left for school in the mornings, and home when I returned. He hung around the house all day, watching cable news or reading the paper. Once I found him alone on the glassed-in sundeck, staring out the window at the bare winter trees. "You know," he told me, "I dread the spring. It's the bleakest time of year."

I wanted to flee, but that would only make things worse. "Why?" I asked fearfully. "What's wrong with spring?"

"False expectations," Dad said. "It leads you to think life is a bunch of daffodils."

The more Dad stayed at home, the less we saw of Mom. She asked her boss to let her put in overtime; we needed the extra money. She didn't come home for dinner most nights. She left meals for us to heat in the mike.

"I don't believe it's about money, though," Caitlyn confided one night, arranging her hair at her bedroom mirror. "She stays away because this house is depressing."

"It *does* remind me of a tomb," I said. "I feel like laughing is a capital crime."

"Get used to it," Caitlyn said. "It'll be like this till Dad finds a job."

"It isn't fair!" I burst out. "Parents are supposed to act like grown-ups! They're supposed to have it together."

"They're human, just like us," Caitlyn pointed out. "You can't expect them to be perfect."

I hated it when she tried to sound full of wisdom, just because she was four years older than I was. "Okay," I said, "but humans don't have to sulk."

"Nobody's sulking," Caitlyn said impatiently. "They're just depressed. Thinking, Why did this have to happen to us?"

"Whatever," I said. "It looks like sulking to me."

But I knew Caitlyn was right. It hurt to think of Dad marched out the door by security guards, as if he'd been caught shoplifting. I hated to think of him and Mom worrying about mortgage payments and health insurance and payments on the car. If only we could find our way back to the smoother, simpler time before all the trouble began.

Regrettably, our bumpy, uneasy way of life had come to stay. As the weeks passed, I almost got used to the new schedule at home. But I never grew accustomed to the silence. Sometimes it felt as though silence hung over us even when we talked.

The only glad note was the superbug. It was gone. Where and why it had vanished didn't matter. My illness was a thing of the past, and I happily put it behind me. At school I was as busy as I'd ever been. I organized the French Club trip to a foreign film festival in Chicago, and worked on the stage crew for *Pygmalion*. I liked working props and painting sets, but acting was my real pleasure. Now that I felt better, I decided to try out for the next production, *The Sound of Music*.

Every day at lunch I kept a lookout for Todd Bowers. Sometimes I caught a glimpse of him, laughing with his friends, or hurrying out the door. Sometimes I imagined running after him, calling, "Todd! It's me! Remember?" But I only watched him from a distance, and wondered, and kept hoping.

One Saturday morning I woke with a dank, heavy feeling all through my body. When I turned over to look at the clock, my hips and shoulders gave a twinge of protest. I had felt those twinges before.

Don't give in to it, I warned myself. I stumbled out of bed and took a long, steaming shower. Not even the stinging hot water brought me back to myself. I felt shaky and tired, as though I hadn't slept all night.

The superbug had returned.

I thought of calling Dr. Pat, telling her I wouldn't be in this morning. It would be delicious to collapse into bed again, to let the long day slip by without me. *Don't let it control you,* I told myself sternly. *It went away before, it'll go away again if you ignore it!*

To my dismay, The Shelter was especially busy. I gave baths to a litter of five spotted puppies that looked to be part Dalmatian. A little girl and her mother came in and adopted a kitten. I tried to persuade them to take two, since we had a major kitten overflow, but the mom wouldn't budge. Finally Dr. Pat put me to work stuffing envelopes for our spring funding drive. I was grateful for the chance to sit down. I didn't think I could stay on my feet another minute.

Even stuffing envelopes was a daunting task.

We were sending out three thousand solicitations. Each envelope had to contain one full-color brochure, one "plea for help" letter, and one return envelope. I arranged the items in neat stacks on the desk and got started. In moments it was clear that I couldn't work from my chair. I needed to step back and forth, reaching, stuffing, stacking. For hours I crossed and re-crossed the office, emptying one carton, filling another, with no end in sight.

On an ordinary day, my hands would have discovered a rhythm to the work, leaving my mind free to wander. Today, it took all my energy just to keep moving. Once Dr. Pat peeked in, eyed the towers of empty envelopes before me, and disappeared again, shaking her head. Her unspoken question hung between us: why was this taking so long?

The door opened, triggering a burst of barking from the kennel. I looked up, hoping we were not about to inherit yet another batch of homeless kittens. For an instant I felt a glow of relief; the figure in the doorway was empty-handed. Then I saw who it was. I froze, my hand in midair.

"Hi, Chloe," said Todd.

"Hi," I said. My voice came out in a squeak. "How's Mocha?"

Talk about a totally uncool thing to say! *Hi, how's your little brother's dog?* I wished I could crawl into one of Dr. Pat's desk drawers.

Todd laughed. "Oh, she's fine! Chewing her way through the house. Last night she ate my new tennis shoes."

"Has she got some chew toys?" I asked. "Dr. Pat always says it helps if you give them something they're allowed to gnaw on." This was going from bad to worse! Every time I opened my mouth a string of clueless words tumbled out.

"Yeah, she's got her rubber bone and her stuffed mouse," Todd said. "She just forgets a lot."

There was an awkward pause. Todd's glance traveled around the room, as though he were looking for a conversation topic.

"Did you want to see Dr. Pat?" I asked.

"No, not really. I was just in the neighborhood. I thought I'd say hello."

"You were in the neighborhood?" I repeated mindlessly.

"Yeah. I've got to get some stuff for my dad at the hardware store. You know—elbow brackets."

Elbow brackets. My brain replayed the words, but they weren't making sense.

"So—you volunteer over here or what?" Todd was asking.

I found my voice again. "No. I get paid."

"Cool!"

"It is. I mean, I like working here."

Silence engulfed us again. After a long moment, Todd asked, "What do you do, anyway?"

"Oh . . . whatever Dr. Pat needs." On an inspiration, I added, "Want me to show you around?"

Todd brightened. "Sure!" he said. "Give me the grand tour."

Talking was easier as I showed him the examining rooms, the bathing room, the outdoor dog runs. We walked through the cattery, kittens peering at us through the mesh of their cages. Some mewed piteously. Others tried to look fierce, arching their backs and puffing up their tails.

As always, the dogs went wild when I opened the door to the kennel. We walked the row of cages, and I told him about the dogs we passed. "This guy I call Mike. I sure wish somebody'd adopt him! . . . See this pup? He came in that day your brother picked out Mocha. I thought he'd be gone by now. . . . Here's Pins and Needles! What a brat! Dr. Pat says she got loose again yesterday!"

Maybe it was the memory of that chase through the office. Or maybe the long day was finally taking its toll. I swayed on my feet, swept by a sudden wave of exhaustion. I leaned against the wall to steady myself, and tried to go on talking as though nothing was wrong.

Todd was asking me something, but I had missed the question. "Huh?" I said.

"I said, why not just leave her out? Give her the run of the place."

"I don't know," I said. I gazed around the room, searching vainly for a chair, but there was none in sight. If I had to stand up for another second, I was sure I'd collapse. I crouched down and pretended to tie my shoelaces. Go through the motions with the left shoe. Check the right, go through the motions with that one, too. Anything to stay on the floor for another second!

"I like this big old sheepdog!" Todd was saying. "Looks like the one in the Disney movie."

"Yeah," I said. "*The Shaggy Dog.*"

I sat where I was as Todd walked down the row. He didn't seem to notice. I breathed more easily, willing strength back into my legs. In a few minutes, I'd be fine. I'd get up and walk Todd to the door and finish stuffing the envelopes. If I could only rest for a few minutes more . . .

"Chloe?" Todd was bending over me. "Don't you get enough sleep?"

"What?"

"You were out like a light. Didn't you hear me?"

"No. I guess . . . I guess I'm kind of tired."

Mortified, I tried to scramble to my feet. I grabbed a hook that jutted out from the wall and hauled myself upright. The room wobbled, but I hung on.

"Are you okay?" Todd asked.

I nodded. I didn't want to risk words.

"You don't look too good," he said. "You look worse than you did the last time."

The last time! This was a rerun, like an old movie they play over and over on TV. Todd must think there was something the matter with me. How could I convince him I was perfectly fine?

"I was up late," I said. "I'm okay. Really."

I felt his eyes on me as I made my way slowly toward the door. Step by careful step I walked to the front office, where there were plenty of seats. Chairs for both of us. I dropped onto the first one in reach.

Todd crossed to the door. He looked back at me with a puzzled frown.

"Well," he said at last, "I'd better go."

"The hardware store," I said, as if he needed a reminder. "Elbow brackets."

"Right. See you at school."

"See you," I echoed.

He waited, and I knew this was my chance. Now, in this instant, I could say something to let him know. If only I could find the right words, and say them in just the right way!

What did I want to tell him, anyway? What made my heart race like this, what made my hands start to tremble? How could I possibly say that, when I saw him, I felt shaky inside?

" 'Bye," he said one last time. In the next moment he was gone, the door swinging shut behind him.

I was still hunched on my seat, half-dozing, when Dr. Pat came in twenty minutes later. I jerked awake guiltily. The stack of empty envelopes loomed on the desk, as tall as it had been the last time she'd looked.

"You're not feeling well, are you?" Dr. Pat said. It was a statement, not a question.

"No," I said miserably. "I guess I'm sick again."

"See if your mom can pick you up," she said, handing me the phone.

"She's out," I said. "Maybe Dad."

"No point in your staying here," Dr. Pat went on. "You belong in bed."

"I know."

Dad arrived fifteen minutes later. He actually seemed pleased at having something to do. He came in and talked cheerfully with Dr. Pat about the nasty bugs going around this year. Finally I stretched my stiff muscles and wobbled out to the car. Dr. Pat watched from the doorway. "Take care of yourself, Chloe," she said, and I heard an anxious note in her voice. "Try to take care!"

4

That night I sat on the couch in the den, bundled in a quilt, even though Caitlyn insisted the room wasn't cold. I didn't like the movie we were watching; it was Caitlyn's choice, something about a girl emigrating from Ireland. Even arguing about the channel took effort. I had no energy to spare.

When the phone rang, I didn't move. I let Caitlyn pick it up, hoping it would be for her.

Caitlyn listened for a moment, then handed the phone to me. I heaved myself upright, trying to ignore the aches in my joints.

"Chloe?" It was Dr. Pat. I thought of those envelopes I'd abandoned, and felt a stab of guilt.

"Hi," I said. I waited for her to go on.

"I just called to ask how you're feeling," she said. "Are you okay?"

There it was, that question again! "It's this bug I keep getting. It'll go away."

"Well, I hope so. Listen, is your mom around?"

"Yeah," I said, reluctantly. "She just got home."

"Great! Let me say hello to her, okay?"

I staggered to the door and called Mom, who picked up in the kitchen. As I hung up the extension, I overheard Dr. Pat saying, ". . . just that I'm concerned . . ."

Why did I suddenly feel apprehensive? Knowing Dr. Pat, there were probably dozens of things she was concerned about, things that had nothing at all to do with me. Still, she had wanted to check up on me. If Dr. Pat was worried about me, I might have good reason to worry about myself.

Ten minutes later, Mom appeared in the doorway. "Dr. Pat sent you home sick again," she said accusingly. "Your father says you were white as a ghost when he picked you up."

"I was a little dizzy, that's all."

Mom came in and put her hand on my forehead. Her fingers felt icy cold, as if she'd been out in the wind with no gloves.

"You feel chilly?" she asked, eyeing the quilt.

"She wanted to turn up the thermostat," Caitlyn put in. "It already says 71."

Mom frowned. "I don't like the way this bug keeps coming back," she said, half to herself. "We'd better check it out."

"You mean make a doctor's appointment?" I asked.

"I'll call Monday morning," Mom said. "Maybe he can take you right away."

"Think he'll give me another antibiotic?" I asked hopefully.

"I would think so. You need to knock this out of your system once and for all."

Caitlyn held a magazine up before her face like a shield. "Don't give your germs to me!" she cried. "I've got a paper due Thursday."

"If my germs were interested in you, you'd have them by now," I pointed out. "They've been around for months."

It felt weird going with Dad to see Dr. Stanley. But since Mom was at work and Dad was home, downsized, it made sense for him to drive me to my appointment that Monday afternoon. Dr. Stanley's office was in the medical building at the shopping mall. We arrived fifteen minutes early, and I killed time browsing through the outlet store on the first floor. The selection was hopeless. I walked up and down the aisles and didn't see a thing worth trying on.

"You don't look like a sick kid to me," Dad remarked as we went up in the elevator. "You've got energy when it comes to shopping."

"I feel better this afternoon," I said. "I had a headache all day in school, though."

"That's school for you," Dad said. I knew he didn't take my aches and pains very seriously. Maybe he was right; maybe they were all in my head. But how could I dream up the stiffness in my shoulders and knees? How could my mind make me shiver with cold when everyone else was toasty warm?

Dr. Stanley's receptionist took my name and said we'd have a bit of a wait. I leafed through a magazine, trying not to think about the ordeal ahead. I hated going to doctors, being probed and studied. I always dreaded the news that something was wrong, something that would require nasty-tasting medicine. But this time I wanted to come. If a pill would make me feel like my old self again, I wanted that prescription!

"Chloe Peterson?"

I started to my feet. Dad waved as I headed for the door. "Catch you later!" he called, as if I were on my way to the supermarket.

"Room 6-A," the receptionist said behind me. A nurse waylaid me en route, and ordered me to stand on a scale in stockinged feet. After she wrote my height and weight down on her clipboard, she ushered me into the examining room and gathered more numbers—blood pressure, pulse rate, temperature. I was being processed like a plucked chicken on a conveyor belt.

I'd only seen Dr. Stanley twice before—a year ago, when I sprained my ankle skiing, and then in January, for my strep throat. I was certain he didn't remember me as he breezed into the examining room, tossing a cheerful "Hi there!" in my direction. He peered into my eyes, had me "open wide" for a look at my tonsils, and listened to my heart and lungs. Then he sat down across the room to talk.

"So, what brings you here today?" he began briskly. "Anything bothering you?"

"No," I said, suddenly confused. "I mean, yeah, sometimes."

"Sometimes? When?"

How could I answer that? I might wake up with a pounding headache, and feel fine by lunchtime. I might be dizzy all afternoon, and recover as I sat doing my homework. I might feel tired for three days, and suddenly, briefly, find my energy restored. "I don't know," I said. "Just sometimes."

Dr. Stanley frowned. He had a thin, serious face with lines that looked as though he frowned a lot. "Okay, can you tell me what feels bad on these sometimes?"

"My head hurts," I said. "My muscles ache. And I get really tired."

"How late do you stay up at night?" he asked.

"I don't know. It depends."

"Pretty late, I bet."

"Sometimes." There it was, that word again!

"So, you're up till midnight, and then you feel tired next day in school, is that it?" Dr. Stanley asked knowingly.

"Not always!" I protested. "I'm not always tired."

"I bet you're a very busy young lady, am I right?" he went on. "Off with your friends, running around with school projects, clubs—have I got the picture?"

I nodded. "I *am* pretty busy," I agreed. "I've got Drama Club and stuff like that."

"Maybe you're so busy you're afraid you can't get everything done. You get worried about all your commitments. You tense up."

"You mean it's stress?" I demanded.

"You find that hard to believe?" Dr. Stanley asked, tilting back in his chair.

"Sometimes I have a fever. Can stress do that?"

"Well, you can get run-down. Then you pick up whatever bugs are going around."

"Can you give me something to get rid of the bug?" I asked, half-pleading.

Dr. Stanley shook his head. "Everybody wants a magic bullet," he sighed. "Too fat, they want diet pills. Too skinny, they want steroids. Too tired, they want pep pills." I opened my mouth to protest, but he went on. "You look to me like a very healthy young lady. Everything's normal. The only thing you need is a little more sleep. Take it easier; it'll do you a world of good!"

"No antibiotic?" I asked.

"No!" he said impatiently. "You don't take antibiotics unless you're sick!"

"But I really do feel sick," I insisted. "Sometimes."

"Listen," Dr. Stanley said, "do you take vitamins?"

"Once in a while."

He smiled for the first time. "Here's what you do," he said. "Go buy yourself a good multivitamin, and take it with your cereal every morning."

"Will that help?" I asked. It couldn't be so easy. It just couldn't!

"No," he said. "It won't. Not unless you get your seven or eight hours of sleep at night, and eat a decent diet, and cut back on your stress level. Forget magic bullets. You've got to change your lifestyle."

He stood up, letting me know I was dismissed. I got to my feet and followed him out the door. In the hall he told Dad, "It's what we see with teens all the time. They get anxious, run-down, they start to not feel well."

"She came down with something just in time for finals after Christmas," Dad said. "You figure that can contribute?"

"You better believe it," Dr. Stanley said. "I see it every semester. Finals Frenzy." Their voices bounced back and forth over my head, as if I wasn't there at all.

"Get her to take vitamins," Dr. Stanley called as he turned away. "One a day."

"See?" Dad said as we went down in the elevator. "Nothing to worry about. You're perfectly okay."

"I guess so," I said uncertainly. Why didn't I feel relieved? Why did I wish Dr. Stanley had asked more questions, given me time to explain? Why did I feel more worried than ever?

As we stepped out of the elevator, my head began pounding once more.

Dr. Stanley was right about one thing—vitamins didn't help much. He was wrong about sleep. I didn't stay up late any more. I had no choice. Sometimes I was so exhausted, I folded at 9:30. No matter how many hours I slept, I woke drained of energy. I dragged through the next week, barely managing classes and homework. I skipped two twirling practices, and Ms. Baker threatened to throw me off the squad. I felt as unreliable these days as Megan McAllister.

Then, on a Monday morning, I awoke feeling well again. I stood up carefully, testing my arms and legs, marveling that I could bend and stretch without pain. Maybe those multivitamins had kicked in at last! Maybe I'd finally logged enough sleep time to satisfy my over-stressed system. Whatever had made the difference, I was grateful.

Gratitude was exactly the word. I was thankful to run for the school bus and spring up the high step without wincing. I relished climbing the stairs to my homeroom on the second floor. I was even thrilled to be wide awake in English Lit class for the first time in days. Mrs. Brinkerman (Mrs. B., as her students called her) was my favorite teacher. I had gotten to know her because she also supervised the Drama Club. She was little and quick, darting back and forth in front of the room as if she could keep the discussion moving with her ceaseless energy.

We were on seventeenth-century poetry now. I focused all my attention on the discussion, eager to capture every word. Toward the end of the period, Mrs. B. remarked, "I think we'll get a clearer idea what Robert Herrick is saying when somebody reads this poem aloud. Chloe, would you do the honors?"

I glanced around, fighting down my embarrassment. Across the room, Sam gave me a sympathetic nod. I drew a deep breath and began:

" 'Gather ye rosebuds while ye may,
Old time is still a-flyin':
And this same flower that smiles today,
Tomorrow will be dying.' "

I finished the last stanza just as the bell rang. I was heading for the door when Mrs. B. called, "Have you got a minute, Chloe? Can I talk to you?"

I paused. "Sure," I said. "My next class is just down the hall."

"You're trying out for *The Sound of Music*, aren't you?" she asked.

My heart leaped. Mrs. B. was the judge at the tryouts, the one who handed out roles. And she was asking, asking *me*, if I was interested!

"I'm planning on it," I said. "Tomorrow, right?"

"Tomorrow at 3:30," she told me. "I hope to see you."

"I'll be there," I promised. "Thanks!"

My backpack was heavy, but I floated to my next class. My feet didn't touch the floor.

Even the elements understood that this was my perfect day. We'd hardly seen the sun in months, but today it shone down like a glowing smile from the heavens. Sam and I took our lunches and joined the swarm of kids outside on the grass. "Hey, look over there," she said with a teasing glint in her voice. I followed her pointing hand. Todd Bowers and a couple of his friends lounged a few yards away. For an instant his eyes met mine. He smiled, and I found myself smiling back.

"Here's a good spot," Sam said, a bit more loudly than necessary. She dropped to the ground and leaned against a tree trunk. I sat beside her, keenly aware of Todd's presence. Should I speak to him, breaking into his conversation with the others? Should I—could I—dare invite him to join us?

Megan McAllister swooped down upon us before I could decide. "Hi, guys!" she crowed as she plopped onto the grass. "I was looking all over for you!"

"What's going on?" I asked.

"I've got to talk to you!" Megan said. "There's something I don't get."

Samantha rolled her eyes. "What now?" she asked.

Megan pulled a crumpled sheet of paper from her purse. "Look at this!" she exclaimed. "Do either of you know how to read a bank statement?"

"Nothing to it, is there?" I asked. "It shows what comes in and what goes out."

"This is so bad!" Megan groaned. "I mean, like I *am* Drama Club treasurer! I'm supposed to get this stuff!"

Samantha rolled her eyes again, to let me know she was in complete agreement. We bent over the statement, studying the columns of figures and lines of fine print. It wasn't quite as simple as I'd expected.

I was actually starting to feel hot. I pulled off my sweater and let the sun pour down on my bare arms. Such glorious weather was unheard-of for the first week in March, and I intended to take full advantage. "You know what this means, don't you?" Sam asked at last. "We're overdrawn by twenty-eight dollars and fourteen cents."

"What's that?" Megan asked fearfully.

"It's as bad as it sounds," I said. "They don't owe us. We owe them."

"The last of the big spenders!" Todd edged closer across the grass, and my heart gave a leap. He must have been listening to everything we said. Listening and watching all along.

"It's for Drama Club," I explained. "The check from the raffle didn't clear in time."

"We can straighten it out, right?" Megan asked anxiously. "Like, it seems like it's all my fault!"

"Go directly to Jail," Todd said. "Do not pass Go. Do not collect two hundred dollars."

The other guys were gathering their books and heading inside. Off in the distance, muffled by the walls, the bell rang.

"I hate to go in!" Samantha moaned. "This is unfair!"

"Hey, I've got my free period next," I said in delight. "I can stay out and tan."

"We'll think of you when we're sitting in Algebra," Megan said.

I waited for Todd to trail after the others. Instead, he settled more comfortably on the grass. Off by the soccer field kids ran and shouted. But their noise seemed far away, disconnected. Right here, right now, it was me and Todd, face to face.

"So," he said.

"So, hi," I said.

For a moment, he looked away. He glanced back at me and smiled. *He doesn't know what to say, I* thought in amazement. *Todd Bowers, who always seems so confident—he's afraid to talk to me!*

Somehow the discovery made him more

human. If he couldn't manage to speak, I could. "What do you think of musicals?" I asked.

"Not a whole lot," he admitted. "My folks dragged me to see *Les Miz*, and it was okay."

"Just 'okay'? I loved it! I wanted to see it again!"

"Weren't you in *Guys and Dolls* last year?" he said. "I went to that."

I nodded. "I'm trying out for *The Sound of Music* tomorrow."

Todd leaned his chin on his hand. "You're brave," he remarked. "Don't you ever freak out up on stage, with everybody looking at you?"

"I hate it for the first minute or two. Then it's easy. Everybody's doing what they're supposed to, and it just works."

"What bands do you like?" Todd asked. That question was a breakthrough. It turned out we both liked Counting Crows. Todd had even been to one of their concerts last summer. Talk about summer led us to talk about winter. I told him about our ski trip to Wisconsin over Christmas last year, and how I managed to sprain my ankle right on the beginners' slope.

When the bell rang, it took me completely by surprise. I couldn't believe we had actually been talking for forty-two minutes.

"Looks like you got sunburned," Todd said as I gathered my things.

"In that little time? I couldn't have!"

"Your face is red," he said. "Your arms, too—look. And on your neck."

Gingerly, I touched my cheek. It stung beneath my fingertips. My head spun when I got to my feet, and my stomach gave a nasty lurch.

I am not going to be sick, I told myself. *I am not going to faint. I am going to make Todd believe I'm perfectly all right.*

Perfectly all right, I repeated to myself. *I'm doing fine. There's not a thing wrong with me.* Inside the building, my head swam, and the floor seemed to roll beneath my feet. It should have been a relief to get under a roof, out of the sun's reach. But I was burning hot, as though it had followed me through the door.

"I go this way," Todd said at a branch in the corridor. "See you."

"See you," I echoed. He waved as he rounded the corner. I felt a little spark of triumph. I had pulled it off. He hadn't guessed how badly I was feeling. As far as Todd Bowers could tell, I was perfectly all right.

6

"**N**obody gets sunburned in March!" Caitlyn informed me. "It's physically impossible."

"Look at my arms!" I moaned. They were covered with angry red blotches from elbow to wrist.

"You look burned, all right," Caitlyn admitted. "But it doesn't make sense. It was sixty-three degrees out!"

"What do you call this?" I stared into the bathroom mirror at the most compelling evidence of all. My face gazed back, red and swollen. A blistered patch crossed the bridge of my nose and spread down over both cheeks.

"That's the weirdest rash," Caitlyn agreed. "You know what it looks like? A butterfly."

"What are you talking about?" Even as I spoke, I saw what she meant. The redness formed a narrow band where it crossed my nose, like a butterfly's slender body. On either side it widened to a pair of wings.

"It's sunburn," I said. "I got it on the lawn outside the caf yesterday."

"Looks to me like you're allergic to something," Caitlyn said, peering more closely.

"Whatever it is, it's ugly!" I told her. "I can't go to school like this! And I've got my tryout today!"

"We can take care of it, never fear!" Caitlyn sounded almost gleeful. She loved rising to a challenge. I watched as she assembled an array of tubes and brushes on the sink counter. Like an artist, she set to work. She began with broad, sweeping strokes, then moved into finer detail. Her touch was featherlight, but I winced all the same.

"Hold still!" she protested. "I'll mess up if you jump around."

I did my best not to move, but the pain was almost more than I could bear. Still, it was worth it in the end. By the time Caitlyn added her finishing touches, the butterfly had disappeared beneath a mask of creams and shadings. My complexion looked clear and healthy once more.

"A masterpiece!" Caitlyn declared, stepping back to gaze at me. "Nobody will ever know!"

"I will, though," I said, sighing. "I'll be worrying all day."

"What for?" Caitlyn asked. "Haven't you ever had a rash before? It's no big deal."

"I know, but . . ." I hesitated. "It's one more thing, that's all."

Caitlyn shrugged. "Hey, we've got to get moving," she said. "Are you watching the time?"

I glanced at my wristwatch. I had to be out the door in fifteen minutes.

"Yeah," I assured her. "I'll make it." I should have gone down to the kitchen for some breakfast, but I wasn't a bit hungry. My stomach felt queasy and uncertain. My legs were heavy, as if my shoes were full of sand.

Caitlyn turned her attention to her hair. "What are all these 'things' you're worried about?" she asked, untangling the cord of her blow-dryer.

"The way I feel lately. I'm fine for a couple of days, and then, *wham!* It's like getting hit by a truck!"

"You taking your vitamins?" she asked.

"Of course!" I said. "Every day!" Caitlyn could be so annoying sometimes! Just because she went to community college, she thought she knew everything.

"Well," she said, fluffing her bangs, "Dr. Stanley says you're fine."

"I know. Only . . ."

"Only what?"

"I should be over this by now, don't you think?"

"Oh, Chloe, there's nothing the matter with you! Don't be a hypochondriac!"

"You mean one of those people who pretends they're sick all the time?"

"They don't pretend. They believe it. They totally talk themselves into it! They get secondary gratification."

"What's that?" I asked suspiciously, edging toward the door.

"We had it in psych class the other day. It's like when you're sick, everybody showers you with attention, and you get out of things you want to get out of—you can lie around and be pampered. It's great."

"Is that what you think I'm doing?" I demanded, stung.

"It isn't conscious," Caitlyn said hastily. "It comes out of your unconscious mind."

"I feel crummy," I said. "There's nothing unconscious about it."

I gulped my vitamin dutifully, but decided to skip breakfast. Hoisting my backpack, I made my way slowly out to the bus stop at the corner. Had I really sprinted down the block just yesterday, the backpack bouncing on my shoulders? The memory felt dim and distant, like something I had only imagined.

With each passing moment, Caitlyn's words hurt more. No one understood how badly I felt—not Mom and Dad, not the doctor, not even my own sister. Did Caitlyn really think I would convince myself that I had headaches and stiff joints, just to gain attention? Did she believe my tiredness was only a ploy to get out of cleaning my room? Did she actually think this "secondary gratification" applied to me?

Today a gray layer of fog hid the sun. The warm spell was over. Late-winter gloom had closed in again. I welcomed the fog as if it were a protective blanket. The sun had singed me, blistered me, and caused me this searing pain. The fog was my ally this morning. The sunshine was my enemy.

Never before had I lived through such a long day at school. By third period I stopped looking at the clock, knowing it would disappoint me. Doggedly, I sat through class after class, willing the minutes to slip away. I was sure I had a fever. My whole body was burning-hot. Then suddenly I was shivering, as though the windows were open to the March winds.

By the end of fourth, I knew I couldn't face the cafeteria. I stumbled down to the nurse's office and asked Mrs. Smalley to let me go home. She took one look at me and picked up the phone, not even bothering to take my temperature. "There's no answer," she said after a long wait. "Can I reach one of your parents at work?"

I remembered Mom and Dad discussing their plans last night, but I hadn't paid attention. Now I tried to think back. "Dad has a job interview," I said. "Mom's got a meeting somewhere outside the office."

Mrs. Smalley frowned. "Isn't there anyone else I can contact?" she asked.

I couldn't think and stand up at the same time. I sagged onto a chair and rested my head in my hands. "Nobody," I said. "I don't think so."

Mrs. Smalley leaned over me. Her voice quivered with distress. "You'd better lie down, honey," she said. "Come with me. You'll be fine."

"Can't I just stay here?" I asked faintly. "This chair's okay."

"There's a nice cot in the other room," she coaxed. "You can rest till your parents get home."

She held out her hand and half-lifted me to my feet. Pushing through a curtained doorway, she led me to a cot. "Here you go," she said. "You make yourself comfy, and I'll take your temp."

Another fit of shivering seized me as I dropped onto the cot. Mrs. Smalley brought a blanket and folded it gently around me. I'd have to tell Joni Schubert, I thought as I floated toward sleep. Mrs. Smalley never once mentioned a Band-Aid.

"Chloe! Chloe! Wake up, dear!"

In those first fuzzy moments, I didn't recognize the face above me. I had no idea where I was or how much time had passed. I sat up dizzily and pulled the world into focus. I was in a room with a green curtain across the doorway. Mrs. Smalley pressed one of those instant thermometers into my ear.

"What time is it?" I asked.

"School's out. The 3:00 bell rang," she said. "Your mother's on her way to pick you up."

"You got her?" My brain worked in slow motion. From a distance, I observed it trying to process each bit of fresh information.

"One-oh-one," Mrs. Smalley said, dropping the used thermometer into the wastebasket. "That's better. It was almost a hundred and three before."

"It's after three o'clock?" I repeated. "Oh, no!"

I scrambled up from the cot. For a moment I wavered, struggling to catch my balance. Then I swung through the curtain and headed for the hall.

"Wait! Chloe, where are you going?" Mrs. Smalley cried at my back.

"I have to go to the tryout," I told her.

"Tryout? You're not trying out for anything today, young lady! Sit down and wait for your mother!"

I heard her, but I didn't have time to take in her words. In my fevered state I could only hang on to one idea at a time. Today was the tryout for *The Sound of Music*. I wanted a part. I'd promised Mrs. B. I *had* to be there.

Mrs. Smalley pursued me into the corridor. It was full of noise and people. Lockers banged, kids laughed and called to each other. Someone bumped into me and almost knocked me off my feet, but I kept going. The auditorium was just around the corner.

Mrs. Smalley put her hand on my shoulder. "Calm down!" she pleaded. "Come and wait in my office."

"Leave me alone!" I exclaimed, shaking her away. "I've got to go!"

She retreated, and somehow I reached the auditorium. People were gathering already, thirty or more. Naturally, there were twice as many girls as guys—that's how it always worked at tryouts. I found the sign-up sheet and added my name. My handwriting looked shaky, as if it wasn't my own.

I took a seat in the front row. As I listened to Mrs. Brinkerman's instructions, I started to feel more awake and aware. We shouldn't be nervous, she told us. We should sing out, not be shy. The play was a comedy; we should try to bring out the humor. A blond sophomore handed out copies of the script. I glanced through mine and decided I'd like to be Liesl, the oldest von Trapp daughter. It wasn't the lead role, but it had a great duet.

Mrs. Brinkerman began calling on people to read. The first girl, Crystal something, stared at her feet and couldn't reach the high notes. Watching her gave me confidence. I knew I could do better than that, even if I was running a temperature! Next came Andy Covo. He had been in *Guys and Dolls* with me last year, and he was good. I was certain he'd get a part this time around, too.

"Who wants to go next?" Mrs. B. asked, looking us over.

Mom would be here any minute. I didn't have much time left. I raised my hand. "I'd like to try Liesl's part," I said when Mrs. B. gave me the nod.

"Good," she said. "Come on up. You and Andy can do the song."

"Sure!" Luck was with me!

I hadn't exactly forgotten that I was sick, but for a few minutes I hadn't remembered it, either. The truth swept in upon me the moment I stood up. Fighting waves of dizziness, forcing my aching body to obey me, I climbed the steps to the stage. I'd never noticed how hard it is to climb stairs without a railing. I longed to hold on to something solid. But nothing was there—nothing but my sheer will to reach the top.

On stage at last, I found my place in the script and read the opening lines. As the piano sounded the first chords of the duet, I scanned the audience for my mother's face. Mom wasn't there. But smiling encouragement from the fourth row was Todd Bowers.

Had Todd decided to try out for the play? No—he wasn't interested in theater, he had told me so yesterday. Then why was he here this afternoon? Had he come just to see me?

I had no time to ponder. Andy Covo was singing the first lines, and in a moment it was my turn to join in. I drew a deep, quavering breath, and began.

I couldn't count on my body, but my voice was still my own. I felt Liesl's spirit, full of innocence and hope, planning a future she thought she could control.

"Fine. You can sit down," Mrs. Brinkerman said at the close. Her tone revealed nothing. I couldn't tell if she liked my performance or not. That was her way—trying to give a fair chance to everyone.

I looked out at the audience again. Todd lifted his hand in a high five. I waved back, glowing with pleasure. Now I knew why he was here. I knew for certain, without a word spoken between us.

I handed the script to Mrs. Brinkerman and started down the steps. Climbing down was harder than going up. My knees wobbled with the effort. If only there was a railing! If only . . .

I don't know precisely when I lost my balance. I just remember the sickening sensation of tilting forward, grappling with empty air, and meeting the floor in a tangle of flailing arms and legs. There were gasps of horror, someone shrieked, and then voices shouted back and forth all around me. I gazed up at a ring of frightened faces.

"I'm all right," I said. "Don't worry about me! I'm fine!"

I wasn't fooling anybody. My shoulder throbbed. Something had happened to my right shin and my left ankle. I struggled to sit up.

The crowd parted to let Mom through. I wondered dimly where she had been waiting. Had she seen me try out? Or had she only seen me fall?

Todd saw me fall, too. He saw my mother

rushing to collect me. He heard the shouts, and saw me splayed out on the floor.

This was, without a doubt, the worst moment of my entire life.

"Chloe!" Mom cried, and her face was white. "What happened? What's wrong? Chloe!"

7

~~~~

"Nothing's broken," I insisted as Mom hustled me out to the car. "See? I can walk!"

Mom didn't buy it. She kept talking about X rays and Ace bandages. I knew the physical damage from the fall wasn't serious: I had a collection of bruises and I'd twisted my ankle. My pride was the part that really hurt. The horrified gasps, the shriek, the cries of dismay ran and reran through my head. I had tried out for a play and created high drama all by myself. And Todd had seen me. I could have borne anything else but that! What had ever possessed him to come to the tryout? Why, oh why hadn't he stayed away?

Back at home, Mom went into high gear. She sent me off to bed and scurried around making tea, toast, and beef bouillon. I was almost asleep when she tapped at my door and came in with a tray. I sat up and balanced my supper on my lap.

"Dr. Stanley is supposed to call back," Mom said. "We've got to get to the bottom of this."

"Of what?" I asked, sipping my tea. Mom had stirred in milk and a teaspoon of sugar, just the way I loved it.

"Of why you can't shake this bug. You've been sick on and off since—" She broke off suddenly and bent closer. "What's that?" she exclaimed. "That rash on your cheeks?"

Instinctively, I spread my hands to hide my face. But it was too late. Caitlyn's cover-up had faded in the course of the day. I didn't need a mirror to know that my strange butterfly had not flown away.

"How long have you had this rash?" Mom demanded. "Why didn't you tell me?"

"I got too much sun yesterday," I protested weakly. "I'm not used to it, it's been so long."

"Sunburn doesn't look like that," Caitlyn said from the doorway. "I told her this morning."

"If you saw she had it this morning, why didn't you say something?" Mom shot back.

"Would you have listened?" Caitlyn asked. "You were rushing around to get out the door!"

Mom's hands fell to her sides. "No," she said in a low, tired voice. "I might not have taken the time. You're right."

"Hey, you don't need to feel bad about it," I put in. "It's just a rash!"

"I don't like the looks of it," Mom said. "I wonder what Dr. Stanley will say."

"It isn't normal," Caitlyn put in. "Nobody gets sunburned in March!"

I woke to the ringing of the telephone. My door was ajar, and I heard Mom answer down the hall. "Oh, Dr. Stanley!" she exclaimed. "I really need to talk to you about Chloe!"

I glanced at the clock next to my bed. Eight-thirty. I must have slept another three hours! How could I sleep all evening, when I'd already slept away the afternoon in the nurse's office?

"Well, no. Not really," Mom was saying. "We're getting kind of worried. The nurse called from school. . . . She's been running a temperature, and—" Her voice dropped to a murmur, and I couldn't catch her next words. There was a pause, and then Mom exclaimed, "No! Nothing like that, but—" and lowered her voice again.

Nothing like what, I wondered. What had Dr. Stanley suggested?

I slipped out of bed and padded to the door in my bare feet. "She sleeps all the time. She's asleep right now," Mom said. "Do you think she could have mono?"

The pause was longer this time. I strained to listen, but Mom wasn't saying a word. I shivered and thought of retreating to my cozy bed. But they were talking about *me!* I had to know what was going on.

"Actually," Mom said, "there is one more thing. She's got a terrible sunburn. . . . Yes, just that little bit of sun we had yesterday. She couldn't have been out long—an hour, hour and a half maybe. It shouldn't affect her like that."

I glanced down at my arms. They were still red and splotchy. "It's on her arms," Mom said, as if she were reading my mind. "Some on her neck. And her face—she has a funny rash. Across her nose, and on her cheeks, too. . . . It's very red and blistered-looking. . . . A butterfly? I hadn't thought of it that way. I guess I see what you mean."

This was the longest pause of all. Maybe Dr. Stanley had put Mom on hold. Fighting dizziness, I leaned against the doorframe for support. I waited. Then Mom's voice exploded into the silence. "The hospital!" she cried. "Don't you want to see her yourself first? . . . Tomorrow morning? The hospital?"

Somehow my shaking legs carried me into the hallway. I met Mom as she was hanging up the phone. "I'm not going to the hospital!" I burst out. "I'm not that sick. I'll be okay if you just let me sleep!"

"Chloe," Mom exclaimed. "I thought you were in bed."

"Why does he want me to go?" I demanded. "What does he want to do to me?"

"He's just trying to be on the safe side," Mom assured me. "He doesn't want to take any chances."

"Chances like what?"

"He says they'll have to run tests. If you're in the hospital, it's easier, he said."

"What kind of tests? What does he think is the matter with me?"

"Chloe, calm down!" Mom said. Her voice was unsteady. She toyed nervously with a notepad on the hall table, looking anything but calm herself.

Caitlyn's door flew open, flooding the hall with music from her CD player. "What's going on?" she asked over the noise, just as Dad appeared at the top of the stairs. Suddenly we were all crowded together, like football players in a huddle, trying to understand, searching for what to do next.

"We have to take you to the city tomorrow morning," Mom told me. "You've got to be at Hamilton by eight."

"I don't know about this Dr. Stanley," Dad said. "Last week he wouldn't even give her an antibiotic, and now he says it's a crisis. Same kid, same problems—I don't get it."

"It's the rash," Mom said. "When I mentioned her rash, he got serious."

I turned my gaze helplessly from one to the other. My family, these people I'd known and relied upon all my life, gazed just as helplessly back. "Do I really have to go?" I asked.

"I guess you do," Dad said. "We better do whatever the doctor says."

We left for Chicago at five the next morning. The drive through rush-hour traffic lasted almost two hours. Getting admitted to the hospital—waiting in lines, filling out endless forms—took an hour more. Finally, Dad took me up to my room while Mom stayed downstairs, arguing about health insurance. There was some mix-up about our policy being transferred over to Mom's name after Dad lost his job.

Everyone's temper was frayed. Mom and Dad spoke to each other in clipped, directed sentences that zinged around my head like bullets. I was glad to get out of the cross fire.

Now I stood in my new room at Alice Hamilton Hospital, weary and confused, my overnight bag at my feet. My brain had gone into slow motion again. I couldn't think what to do next. I waited for someone to give me instructions.

Dad tried to lighten my mood. "Come here," he urged. "Look outside. Your view is totally cool." Grown-ups should be content to talk like grown-ups. It always made me cringe when my parents tried to sound like kids. Obediently, I joined Dad at the window. Lake Michigan spread below us, churned into whitecaps by the wind. Gloom and cold seemed to billow toward me from the choppy water. I shivered and turned away.

"I never realized Hamilton is right on the

lakefront," Dad said. "They've got a fantastic location here!"

He was sounding like a dad again. At least that was an improvement. "I don't care about the location," I said. "It's the ugliest place I ever saw." From the outside, Hamilton looked like a penitentiary—a complex of dingy gray buildings piled together like cell blocks. My room with a view was on D-4. The woman in Admitting told me brightly that I would be in the new Adolescent Wing. She acted as though getting assigned to D-4 was a special privilege.

I was in no mood to be grateful. When a nurse bustled in and handed me a frilly white hospital gown, I barely said thank you.

"Not a happy camper, are you?" she remarked, unperturbed. "You'd rather be somewhere else."

"Any place but here," I grumbled.

"Most of the kids on the unit feel the same way, if that's any consolation," she said. "Let's see your arm—I need to draw some blood."

"They did that already," I protested. "They stuck me downstairs."

"Sorry. We have to have more." I could tell her "sorry" was just a figure of speech. She didn't feel a drop of sympathy. She was a tall, big-boned woman who looked like she should have been mustering troops instead of hovering at bedsides. The name tag on her collar read, "Midge Hazeldorf." The name Midge suggested someone tiny and giggly. For this lady, it was a complete mismatch.

Midge waved me to a chair, and I sat down as directed. Resistance would be useless. She pushed up my sleeve, and I flinched as her hands brushed my sunburn. She studied my blotches for a moment before she plunged in her needle. I clenched my fists in my lap and tried not to make a sound.

"What do they need all this blood for?" I asked as she patted a Band-Aid into place.

Dad drew closer, awaiting a crucial answer.

Midge only shrugged. "Tests," she said. "We'll sit down with you when the results are in."

"What am I supposed to do in the meantime?" My voice rose shrilly. "Just sit around and wait?"

"Oh, we'll keep you busy," she assured me. "And your roommate will be in pretty soon. You'll have someone to talk to."

"Who is she?" I asked.

"You're with Melissa Santiago. She'll tell you who she is."

I still sat in the chair, awaiting the next order.

"Put on your gown and hop into bed," Midge said. "I'll be back when I finish my rounds."

After she bustled out, Dad said he had to be getting along, too. "We'll all come see you tonight," he promised, hugging me good-bye. "After rush hour."

"Mom and Caitlyn, too?" I felt like a little kid, pleading for comfort.

"All of us," Dad repeated. "Take it easy, but take it." It was one of his favorite expressions. Usually it annoyed me, but today, as his back disappeared through the doorway, it made me want to cry.

8

~~~

Late that afternoon, I woke to the murmur of voices nearby. Someone had drawn the curtain around my bed, and I seemed to be lying in a dark cocoon. For a few moments I was too foggy to think. Slowly, the truth sank in again. I was at Hamilton Hospital, waiting. Waiting to find out.

I closed my eyes and tried to retreat back into sleep. I was still tired (I was always tired, wasn't I?) but I was hopelessly wide-awake.

"There you go, honey," a female voice cooed. "Back to your very own bed, nice and cozy."

At last my curiosity broke to the surface. Pushing the curtain aside, I saw a pair of nurses rolling a motionless body from a stretcher onto the empty bed across the room. "So you're awake," one of the nurses greeted me. "This is Melissa, your roommate."

My cellmate, you mean, I wanted to answer. All I could see of Melissa was a swirl of black hair emerging from a nest of blankets. The nurses fussed over her for a few more minutes, and she answered their questions with faint groans. At last the nurses wheeled the empty stretcher away and left Melissa and me alone together.

Melissa did not stir. Through long minutes I watched her for a sign of life. Slowly, a cold fear crept into my chest. Suppose she had died, and nobody knew except me! Suppose I was sharing my room with a corpse!

We made quite a pair, I thought ironically. I knew I didn't look much better than Melissa did. My hair was a wreck, and my face was puffy from sleep and sun rash. I had no energy to move. Here we lay, the two of us, more dead than alive.

Across the room, Melissa emitted a soft moan. With a surge of relief, I craned my neck to get a better look at her. A hand emerged from her blankets. Her head turned, and two sparkling brown eyes met my gaze. She looked to be about thirteen—and very much alive.

"Hi," I said shyly. "I'm Chloe Peterson."

Melissa's only response was another, louder moan.

"You okay?" I asked.

She pushed herself up against her pillows. "What does it look like?" she snapped.

"Sorry," I said. "The second I asked you, I knew it was a stupid question."

"Hey, it's not the stupidest," she said. "When I woke up in Postop yesterday, some resident's trying to be funny—he goes, 'Feel like an ice cream sundae? How 'bout it?' "

Maybe my brain was still fuzzy with exhaustion. The story didn't make sense. "What's Postop?" I asked.

"You know," Melissa said patiently, as though she was much older and wiser. "Recovery. After my operation."

I still wasn't getting it. "Recovery from what?"

Melissa gave up and changed the subject. "Haven't you ever been in here before?"

"No," I said, with a touch of pride. "I've never been in a hospital in my life, except, I guess, when I was born."

"You get born in them and you die in them," Melissa remarked. "That's what my grandmother says."

I didn't like the turn this conversation was taking. For that matter, I didn't much like Melissa. "I'm only here for a day or two," I told her. "My doctor wants me to have blood tests, that's all."

"Oh, yeah?" Melissa asked with interest. "What kind?"

"I don't know," I admitted. "They didn't say yet."

"Have you had a bone marrow?"

"A what?" I thought of the way Caitlyn used to crack open her chicken drumstick and suck the marrow to gross me out. It always succeeded.

"You really *haven't* been here before, have you? A bone marrow's when they drill into your chest with this gigantic needle. It's about this thick." She held up her hand, her thumb and forefinger an inch apart.

"I don't need anything like that," I said hastily. "Just what they call blood work."

Melissa was quiet for a while. I hoped she had gone to sleep again. I closed my curtain and tried to drift off, too.

Suddenly Melissa's voice found me through the darkness. "Don't you hate it when they won't tell you anything? It's always better when you know."

In a rush, I understood why I felt so angry. I was angry with everyone's empty good cheer. I was angry at being locked up away from home. But, most of all, I was angry because no one would answer my questions. They were looking for something with all their tests, some flaw in my body to explain my symptoms. It was *my* body they were investigating—but no one would tell me what might be wrong.

"Chloe?" Melissa whispered. "You awake?"

"I hate it, too," I whispered back. "They ought to tell us. We've got the right to know."

Dad, Mom, and Caitlyn came to see me after supper that evening. Dad and Mom floated in and out of the room, trying to waylay some doctor or other. I'd seen a doctor briefly in the afternoon, a skinny, nervous guy with a mustache. I couldn't remember his name. He was just one more of the people who paraded in and out, pricking, poking, prodding, and asking me the same questions again and again: "How long have you felt tired? . . . Have you ever had swollen glands in your neck? . . . Do your joints ache?" Always they came back to one seemingly crucial point:

"How long were you out in the sun when you got this burn?"

"Hey, look, I brought you a card," Caitlyn said. She had made it on the computer. A kitten with a silly hat and a Cheshire-cat grin said, "Get well quick! Don't miss the party!"

"You still think I'm doing this for secondary gratification?" I asked her, propping the card on my bedside table.

Caitlyn shifted uncomfortably on the chair beside my bed. "I'm sorry," she said. "I guess I've been reading too much psychology."

"I guess you have," I said grimly. "It's no party in here, let me tell you!"

Across the room, Melissa and her grandmother conversed in rapid-fire Spanish. Now and then I picked up a phrase I remembered from Spanish II class. "En casa" was "at home." "Muy enferma" meant "very sick." You didn't need to know the language to tell what people were talking about in this place. It was all sickness, needles, blood, and marrow.

"Well," Mom said as she and Dad came in, "they say it'll be a few days before we know anything for sure. A Dr. Suarez will sit down with us when all the results are in."

Dad stood in his favorite spot, by the window. He couldn't have seen much of a view at this time of day, but he stood there anyway, looking out into the darkness.

"After all the tests, what's this Suarez guy going to tell us?" I asked.

"We'll know when we have the conference!" Mom said irritably.

"You must have some idea what they're looking for," I insisted. "What did they tell you?"

"Don't worry about things that haven't happened yet," Mom said. "Let's keep our fingers crossed."

When I was little, my friends and I used to cross our fingers if we were telling a fib. That way, it wasn't supposed to count as a lie. I pictured this Dr. Suarez, whoever he might be, telling me that I was perfectly all right, with his fingers crossed behind his back.

After everyone went home, the nurses whisked in to check on Melissa and me. They reminded me to press the call button if I needed anything, and told me to go to sleep. The corridor grew quiet. I longed for the sound of a human voice.

"Melissa," I called softly. "Are you awake?"

"Yeah," she said. "Why?"

"That operation you had," I said. "What was it for—did they tell you?"

For a few moments she didn't reply. "Cancer," she said at last. "They took out part of my hip-bone."

Cancer! The word pierced my guts like a knife. Surely that's what I had, too. Now I knew why they had rushed me into the hospital. No wonder they were running endless blood tests. No wonder nobody dared to answer my questions. No wonder I was afraid to ask.

"You have cancer?" I echoed. "Wow! I'm sorry!"

"That makes two of us," Melissa said. "I'm sorry, too."

Somewhere down the hall an alarm went off. I huddled under the covers and listened to the long, shrill blasts of the buzzer. One, two, three times it blared before it broke off as abruptly as it had begun. All around me people were sick, even dying—the adolescents of D-4, kids like me. What was I doing here? Only the day before yesterday I had sat on the grass with Todd. That was my life—to be with my friends, to be busy, to have fun. I didn't belong here! I wanted to go home!

Pretty soon I'd find out this was all a mistake, I promised myself. Dr. Suarez would finally prescribe the antibiotic I should have been taking all along. I would get my energy back. I would bound through the days again, full of life, without an ache or a twinge. Pretty soon this would all be over.

"My pain meds are kicking in," Melissa said. "I'm fading."

"Good night," I said. My words fell into silence. Melissa was asleep.

9

I slept fitfully all night, awakened by strange beeps and crashes, murmurs and cries. Once I thought I heard sobbing from Melissa's side of the room. A nurse spoke in comforting tones. I tried not to wake up enough to listen.

At six in the morning, a red-haired nurse named Kitty woke me to take my temperature and give me a pill. She explained that she was "going off-shift," and wouldn't be back till Sunday, after her days off. "I won't be here," I said firmly. "After we talk to Dr. Suarez, I'm going home."

Kitty glanced at my chart. She looked back at me with a sugary smile. "Well," she said, "if I don't see you again, you take care of yourself!"

"You don't believe me, do you?" I asked her. "You don't think I'm leaving."

"If Dr. Suarez says you're going, you're going," she said. I could make of that whatever I chose.

After breakfast, I switched on the TV and discovered nothing but early-morning cartoons and talk shows. I didn't know how I would get through the day. Melissa was restricted to bed, but I was free to walk around if I felt well enough to get up. "Go down to the lounge," Melissa urged. "You go past the nurses' station and it's around the corner."

"It's got to be better than lying around here watching the soaps," I grumbled. The words were out before I realized how they must sound to Melissa. She didn't want to be stuck in the room either, but she had no choice.

"Go check out who's there," she said. "If you see Cassie, send her down."

"Sure," I said, though I had no idea who Cassie was. I climbed down from my high hospital bed and searched beneath it for my paper hospital slippers. My hospital nightgown, slit up the back and tied with a series of laces, hung limp and shapeless as a sack. My situation had only one redeeming virtue, I thought as I padded down the hall. My friends were far away, back home in Woodstock. None of them could see me now.

It was easy to find the lounge—as soon as I turned the corner past the nurses' station, I heard the music. Cautiously, I peered through the half-open door. Two boys were engrossed in a video game, while a bored-looking girl watched them and polished her nails. The boys both sat in wheelchairs, and the girl was hooked to a contraption with a pole, a hanging bag of clear fluid, and a lot of plastic tubing.

I didn't belong there. This place was for kids who were really sick. It wasn't for people like me, who just needed an antibiotic. I turned to flee, but one of the boys spotted me. "Hey, new girl!" he called. "You scared of us?"

"No," I said. "I just want to walk around, that's all." *There I go again*, I scolded myself. *Wouldn't I ever learn?*

"Come say hi first," the boy said. "I'm Aaron, and this guy's Jack."

Jack said something, but it sounded as if he had a mouthful of marbles. He must have seen my blank expression, because he said it again, louder and more slowly. I still didn't understand a word.

"He said, 'What brings you to this pleasure spot?' " Aaron translated.

"Nothing, really," I said. "I mean, nothing important. I'm tired and I got a really gross sunburn."

"I'll say," said the girl with the pole. "If I got burned like that, I'd hide out in the hospital, too."

"Thanks a bunch," I said. She was a fine one to criticize, wired up like that!

"Well," she said, "you going to come in or not?"

It would be awkward to go in and sit down, but it would be even more embarrassing to walk away. The choice was plain. "I'm Chloe," I said, taking a seat on the sofa. "I just got here yesterday."

"My name's Cassandra Mullins," the girl said. "Everybody calls me Cassie."

"Oh!" I cried. "My roommate told me to look for you. She can't get up yet."

"You mean Melissa? She feels like company? I'll go see her." Cassie had a nice smile, even though she wore braces. She had beautiful long hair, the color they call honey blond.

"Oh, man!" Aaron exclaimed to Jack. "I quit! You win!"

I couldn't understand Jack's words, but there was no mistaking his laughter. "Later, maybe," Aaron said. "I don't want to play anymore right now." Apparently Aaron understood Jack just fine.

The boys left their game and wheeled over to join us. I was the star attraction. They both seemed eager to impress me. Aaron told me he was on a wheelchair basketball team, and Jack (with Cassie translating this time) said he went white-water rafting last summer.

"We went to Wisconsin," I said. "Thrilling, right?"

"You ever notice that about guys?" Cassie asked me. "They're always trying to prove how cool they are."

"You mean girls don't do it, too?" Aaron asked. "Girls are no different, isn't that what you say all the time?"

"We're different when it counts," Cassie said. "Like we can express ourselves better. Right, Chloe?"

"Right," I said. I was hardly a good example. The whole scene was so bizarre, I couldn't think of anything to say. All three of them acted so normal! But they *weren't* normal—you could tell at a glance. I wasn't like them. I didn't need poles and tubes. And I could stand on my own two feet.

After a while, the nurse named Midge came and reminded the boys that it was time for physical therapy. "Already?" Aaron groaned. "Not yet."

"The time is now," Midge said. "Get a move on!"

"You can't argue with the Midget," Cassie told me. "She says it once, and that's it."

"I like that," I said. "The Midget."

Cassie followed me back to the room, wheeling her pole contraption beside her. Melissa broke into a grin when she caught sight of her. I left the two of them chattering away about people whose names I'd never heard of. I paced down the hall in the other direction, away from the nurses' station and the lounge. At the far end was a wide, sunny window filled with hanging plants. I gazed out through the trailing leaves. Below me, the lake stretched as far as I could see. I emptied my mind of thoughts, and watched the waves rise and fall, rise and fall upon the beach.

Nothing gets done in the hospital over the weekend. One delay followed another as we waited for my test results, and my stay at Hamilton stretched on and on. When Kitty returned on Sunday morning, I was still on D-4.

Finally, on Tuesday, our fateful meeting was scheduled. At 4:30, Dad, Mom, and I went to the conference room next to the nurses' station to wait for Dr. Suarez. The room was small and homey, with cushioned chairs around a glass-topped coffee table. Bright pictures hung on the walls—a Mexican market scene, a ship in full sail, a New England snowscape. I wondered how many other kids had waited here with their families, hoping and praying for good news. Had Melissa sat here, and heard in this very room the news that she had cancer? Had Jack and Aaron and Cassie all learned the truth within these four walls?

It was my turn now. I sat silently, my hands locked together in my lap, almost too scared to breathe. I hoped. I prayed. I waited.

By 4:50 there was still no sign of Dr. Suarez. Mom went out to the nurses' station to inquire. Dad seemed uncomfortable when the two of us were alone together. He tried to tell me a joke about a dog and some fleas, but he couldn't re-member the punch line. Mom came back and said the nurse would have Dr. Suarez paged. I said nothing. We waited.

After a while, the Midget came in and assured us that Dr. Suarez was on his way. "Help yourselves to coffee," she urged. None of us moved. Nothing mattered but waiting.

At 5:15, after we'd been waiting forty-five minutes, the door swung open. Dr. Suarez hurried in with a thick blue folder under his arm. I recognized him as the short doctor with the mustache who had questioned me last week. "I'm so sorry to hold you up," he began, setting the folder down on the table. "I was doing a clinic over in the Grafton building, all the way at the other end of the complex."

Dad and Mom assured him it was okay, that they understood. I stared wordlessly at the blue folder. On the front, I read my name, "Chloe Marie Peterson," in big, black letters. My future, my life, lay hidden between those covers.

"So, I'm Dr. Suarez," the doctor went on, as if we hadn't guessed. He shook hands with each of us in turn, and settled down in an empty chair. I noted that he didn't lean back. He perched on the forward edge, as though at any moment he would take flight.

"Okay, let's get started," he said when the introductions were finished. "We have all the preliminary results in. We'll do some further testing, of course, to pin things down for certain, but I can give you as much information as I have."

Mom and Dad murmured their thanks. I sat frozen, unable to twitch a muscle.

"Any time we give families a diagnosis, naturally, everyone gets anxious and worried," Dr. Suarez went on, as though he were delivering a carefully rehearsed speech. "Naturally, it can be frightening when we put a name on a condition, whatever that condition is. Everyone wants to know, what will this mean for the future? Will it get worse? What will the treatment be like? Are they working on a cure?"

"Do you *have* a diagnosis for our daughter?" Dad interrupted.

"As I say, we have the preliminary results," Dr. Suarez said. He had the faintest trace of a foreign accent. You could tell he hadn't grown up in the United States. I wondered what country he came from. Probably someplace where they spoke Spanish. . . .

"Does that mean you're still not sure?" Dad pressed.

"No, I must tell you we *are* clear about the diagnosis itself. The extent of the condition, that is still to be determined. Now, if you will let me speak, please, and ask your questions afterward."

"Okay," Dad said sheepishly. "Go ahead."

Dr. Suarez paused, his gaze traveling to each of us in turn. It rested last upon me. He smiled kindly. Regretfully. A finger of dread crawled down my spine. This was a man who faced the painful task of delivering bad news. He must have done it countless times before, and yet it was always hard.

I have cancer, I thought with a jolt of brutal certainty. *I have cancer, and I'm going to die. I'll never grow up. I'll never drive a car or go to the Senior Prom or live in a college dorm. In another moment, he will say the word, and it will echo in this room where so many other kids have heard terrible news before me. Cancer. Cancer . . .*

"You will have a lot of questions, I am sure," Dr. Suarez resumed. "For now, you just need to take in what I am about to tell you. The tests reveal that your daughter has systemic lupus erythematosus."

"Not cancer?" I exclaimed. A great wave of relief surged up from the soles of my feet. I was free! I had been spared! I would live to grow up after all!

"What does that mean?" Mom asked. "Systemic whatever—I've never heard of it before."

"Sometimes it's called SLE," Dr. Suarez explained. "Most of the time, the disease is simply known as lupus."

Lupus. The name had a dark, sinister sound. It wasn't cancer, I told myself again. But my relief was ebbing away.

Dr. Suarez talked on. "Lupus is what we call an autoimmune disorder. That is to say, the immune system gets confused. It sees the body's own tissue and thinks it's an enemy invader. So it launches an attack and begins to do damage. We say 'systemic' because lupus can attack any organ, any system of the body."

I wanted to say, *Wait! Stop! I can't bear this, don't tell me any more!* But Dr. Suarez went right on talking. "Symptoms may disappear for a while—we say they are under control. Or they will become active, in what we call a flare-up. This flare-up of yours brought you here to the hospital."

Suddenly I heard my own voice, springing forth loud and defiant. "But I won't die from it, right? It isn't like cancer. You don't die!"

Again Dr. Suarez offered me his kind, regretful smile. "Thirty years ago, the odds were not very good," he said. "About half of all lupus patients died within five years." I gasped in horror, but he went on, "Today, we have new drugs that can be very effective. About eighty percent of all patients live ten years or more. Many will have a full life span. The chances for that are very good."

"So, you mean I'll get better?" I asked. "I'll take medicine and I can get rid of this—this disease?" I couldn't bring myself to say the name.

Dr. Suarez shook his head. "Lupus is a chronic condition," he said. "We can control many of the symptoms. But, right now, we do not have a cure. When you develop lupus, you have lupus for the rest of your life."

His hands rested side by side, straight and open upon his knees. If only his fingers were crossed! If only he were telling me a lie!

"But you're saying it's not fatal," Dad said. "Eighty percent chance she'll be okay in ten years."

Dr. Suarez lifted a hand for silence. "Nowadays lupus is not often fatal," he said. "But it *will* affect her quality of life. She may have symptoms that come and go—inflammation of the joints, headaches, nausea, tiredness. Her heart could be affected, or her kidneys. She will have to stay out of the sun. People with lupus can be very sensitive to ultraviolet light. It can cause a dangerous burn and a severe flare-up of other symptoms."

"My sunburn," I said dully. "In March."

"You have the butterfly rash across your nose and cheeks," Dr. Suarez told me. "In lupus, that pattern is seen very often. It is a telltale sign."

"But she will be all right," Dad repeated. "She won't die from this."

"With medical treatment today, it is not so much a question of whether she will die," Dr. Suarez said patiently. "The question really is, What sort of life is she going to live?"

10

~~~~~

I think we sat in the conference room for another half hour. Dad and Mom must have asked some more questions, and Dr. Suarez probably gave them answers. It's all very vague as I look back on it now. Words clattered around me like hailstones, but I couldn't take them in.

Once I looked up at the painting across the room from me—a ship in full sail, rising to the crest of an enormous wave. I noted the detail of the masts and rigging, and the spray splashing over the deck. Here and there small human figures clung to ladders and hauled on ropes. The people in the picture hardly seemed to matter. They were tiny compared with the power of the wind and the waves.

"There have to be new developments out there," Dad said. "There might even be something on the Internet."

"Yes, there is a lot of research in the field," Dr. Suarez agreed. "If I learn of any new treatments, believe me, I'll let you know."

"I'll be checking the Web myself," Dad said. "If I find anything, I'll let *you* know, too."

At last Dr. Suarez gathered up the blue folder. He rose to his feet, letting us know we were dismissed. "Slow down," he said, nodding in my direction. "I cannot emphasize it enough, young lady. With lupus, you will need to take it easy."

I stood up with the others. Dr. Suarez shook hands with each of us in turn. His grip was surprisingly warm and firm. "You will do well," he promised. "Just remember, you *must* rest."

"Can I go home now?" I asked. My voice sounded small and pleading, as if I were a little kid.

"By the weekend," Dr. Suarez said. "When all of your tests are completed."

What was the good of running more tests? I wondered. *They knew what was wrong with me. I had an incurable disease. It would never go away. I would have it as long as I lived.*

* * *

The next morning, the Midget brought me a glass of water and a paper cup full of pills. They were starting me on "a course of medication," as Dr. Suarez had put it, to "get some of the symptoms under control." Not all of the symptoms, I thought grimly—the medication would control only *some*. Nobody could seem to tell me which ones.

"Hey, I brought you a present," the Midget said as I downed the first capsule. "You like comics?"

She handed me a brightly colored comic book with a picture of Little Red Riding Hood on the cover. She was walking through the woods, carrying a basket. In the trees behind her lurked a sinister shadow. The title read: *"Lupus, The Big Bad Wolf."*

"Did Dr. Suarez tell you the word 'lupus' means wolf in Latin?" the Midget asked.

I shook my head. "He didn't tell me anything," I said. That was perfectly untrue. He had told me lots of things. He just hadn't said anything I wanted to hear.

"Well, that little comic book has a lot of information packed into it," the Midget assured me. "Take a look."

"Later," I said. I stuffed the comic into the drawer of my bedside table.

"Hey there, Midget," Melissa called from across the room. "Can you bring me some water when you get a chance?"

"Soon as me and Chloe finish up," the Midget said. She turned back to me. "One more thing, and I'll quit bugging you for a while. We've got a discussion group for kids with lupus and things like that. Chronic diseases. You know—things that last a long time."

"Like forever, you mean," I said.

She ignored my bitter tone. "The group is a place where you can talk to other people who are going through what you are."

"I'm not going *through* anything!" I said. "There isn't any end to it, ever. I'm *always* going to have this disease!"

"You'll have times when you feel fine. Maybe long stretches. You won't always feel sick."

"I'll always be waiting for it to come back," I said. "I won't ever be normal again!"

"It really would help," the Midget began, "for you to drop by the lounge this afternoon. Four o'clock. You know some of the kids already—"

"I don't want to sit around listening to everybody's aches and pains!" I burst out. "I'm fifteen, not seventy-five!"

"Most kids feel that way in the beginning," the Midget said. "You're not the only one, you know."

"We can all be miserable together. How fun!"

"Hey," she said, "if you run out of symptoms to gripe about, you can always complain about us nurses!"

She was trying to cheer me up, but I was in no mood to give her that satisfaction. "I've got a job at the animal shelter," I told her. "You know what happens when we get a cat or a dog with some incurable disease?" Before the Midget could answer me, I raced on. "They get a lethal injection! We put them to sleep! That's what we do for cats and dogs!"

The Midget rested one of her big, wide hands on my shoulder. "I know it's hard. It's going to take you a while to adjust. But you will, you'll—"

"I don't *want* to adjust!" I cried, shaking her hand away. "Why did this have to happen to me? I'd rather be dead!"

"Chloe," the Midget said soothingly. "Chloe."

"I would! I would!" I raged. "If I have to have lupus for the rest of my life, then I'd rather die!"

* * *

When the Midget finally left me alone, I drew the curtain around my bed and burrowed beneath the covers. My thoughts spun round and round, following the same track again and again. I'd always obeyed the rules. I paid attention in class, I turned in my homework on time. I called my parents if I was going to be late. I stayed away from wild parties. I was nice to people. Some people were mean. They spread gossip, cut people down. Why didn't *they* get lupus? Why did I get sick instead of all those others? I didn't deserve this! It wasn't fair!

Someone came into the room. I braced myself for another nurse, more pills and prodding. But the footsteps passed my bed, and a murmur of voices floated from Melissa's side of the room. After a few minutes, I heard someone coaxing Melissa to walk, assuring her that she could manage if she leaned a bit more forward. Once Melissa gave a little cry of pain. There was a lot of rustling and clattering, and at last they were gone. For the first time in days, I was alone.

Sometimes when I was little, I used to have nightmares. I would wake up, quivering with fright, and curl up into a tight ball under the blankets. I thought that if I made myself as small as possible, the monster of my dream would never find me.

Now I drew my knees to my chest and clasped my arms around them. I searched for the comfort I had found through those haunted nights long ago. I folded myself as small as I could, so that I was only a quiet mound under the bedclothes. But it was too late to hide. The wolf had already found me.

Next to my bed the phone rang. I didn't want to speak to anyone. I let it ring once, twice, three times. Finally, on the fourth ring, I pushed back the covers and lifted the receiver. "Hello?" I said.

"Chloe?" It was Sam's voice. "Hey, how are you?"

"I'm okay," I said.

"What do you mean, okay? You've been in the hospital for a week!" In the background, I heard a jumble of voices and the tinkle of silverware. She was calling from the caf. In another life, it was fifth period.

"What did they tell you?" I asked.

"Who? Your mother?"

"Yeah, who else?"

"Oh . . ." Sam hesitated. "She said you've got something with a long name."

"That's what they told us, yeah."

"So, how are you feeling?" Sam persisted. "Are they giving you something?"

"All kinds of stuff. For my symptoms, they say."

"You'll be all right, then," she said, relieved. "You'll be fine."

I didn't answer, and after a moment she went on. "Hey, guess what! You got a part in *The Sound of Music!* You're Liesl!"

For an instant, excitement danced through me. I sat up, kicking free of the covers. I thought of the fun of rehearsals, the shared jokes, the hilarious mistakes, the cast growing closer night after night. I had loved every minute when we put on *Guys and Dolls* last year. And this year I would be part of it again.

Then I remembered my tumble down the steps, my body sprawled on the cold linoleum, everyone surging around me in panic. Why had Mrs. B. given me a part after that? Couldn't she tell I was in no shape to perform before an audience?

"Well, say something!" Sam exclaimed. "Aren't you glad?"

"I can't be in a show," I said dully. "The doctor says I've got to take it easy from now on."

After Sam said good-bye, I called the school

and asked for Mrs. Brinkerman. I knew she'd be in class, and I was glad I didn't have to speak to her in person. I left a message on her voice mail. "Hi, this is Chloe Peterson," I said. "I just heard that I got the part of Liesl. Thank you, but—" A lump caught in my throat, and for a second or two I couldn't say a word. "I'm in the hospital right now, and even when I get out, I'm supposed to rest a lot. So, Mrs. Brinkerman, I'm sorry—I'm not going to be able to take the part. I can't be in the play after all."

I set down the phone and curled up under the covers again. For the first time, I let myself cry. Alone in my high hospital bed, I shook with sobs. My whole life was ruined. Nothing would ever be the same again. There was nothing to look forward to, nothing but lupus with all its misery. The big bad wolf had stolen away my future.

11

I yearned to have familiar things around me, to hear the ordinary sounds of home. Every day I asked how much longer I had to stay at Hamilton, and every day the nurses told me I needed "just a few more tests." They kept me in the hospital through another long, dreary weekend.

On my second Monday afternoon, Dr. Suarez came in, smiling. "I have good news for you, young lady," he announced. "Your lupus has not damaged any of your vital organs. Your tests show your heart, lungs, kidneys, brain—everything is fine."

"But I still have lupus," I said. "Anything can go wrong."

"You're doing extremely well," he assured me.

"It's possible your lupus may remain fairly mild. If you learn to manage your condition, you can live quite normally."

"Can I go back to school?" I asked. I half-hoped he would say no. I didn't want to go back, to face all the anxious questions that awaited me.

"Of course, go to school!" Dr. Suarez exclaimed. "Do all your regular activities. Only in moderation. Always in moderation."

"How do I do school in moderation?" I asked pointedly. "Go on a half-day schedule?"

"Get your homework done early and go to bed."

I knew what came next. "Rest," I said. "Take it easy. Slow down."

The doctor's smile broadened. "You're getting the hang of it," he said. "You'll be fine."

Dad picked me up that evening, to go home at last. Getting discharged was almost as complicated as being admitted. There were forms to fill out and releases to sign. Down at the nurses' station, the Midget handed us a fat manila envelope. It was stuffed with instructions about my medications, advice on diet and exercise, and dire warnings to stay out of the sun. "Your owner's manual," Dad quipped. He turned to the

Midget and asked, "Does she come with a ninety-day warranty?"

I groaned. The Midget winked at me. "You're not funny, Dad," she told him, reading my thoughts.

"Seems like I never am," he said. "Must be my delivery."

"No," the Midget assured him. "It's your age. Just comes with being a parent."

Dad waited while I went back to check my room one last time. In the drawer of my bedside table I discovered the Big Bad Wolf comic book. I glanced around for a wastebasket, but there wasn't one handy. Without thinking, I stuffed the comic into my purse.

I met Melissa in the hall outside our door, practicing with her aluminum walker. "I guess this is good-bye," I said, a little awkwardly. "It's been nice rooming with you." Melissa had been lively and good-natured. She didn't complain much, even when her leg hurt, even though she must have been scared sometimes. Melissa really *was* a good roommate. I wondered if she could say the same about me.

"Maybe I'll see you around," she said. "In out-patient. Or when you come back for the group."

"Don't hold your breath on that one," I said, and gave her a hug. She hugged back and headed down to the lounge.

For a moment I stood still, watching her walk away. *Melissa has cancer,* I thought with a sudden stab. *I might never see her again.*

While I was in the hospital, I had felt like a displaced person. I was in the wrong bed, on the wrong schedule, eating the wrong meals, among the wrong people. I couldn't wait to get home. But once I found myself back in Woodstock, I discovered that being at home wasn't the answer. It was good to be in my own room again, with all its clutter around me. It was good to pop my own snacks into the microwave, and to hear Caitlyn in the den, typing on the computer. But, somehow, I didn't seem to fit in any more. Dad made one desperate joke after another, and Mom was nervous and out of sorts. All evening they hovered over me, asking if I felt all right. They reminded me to take my pills, and insisted that I go to bed by 9:30. I had left home an ordinary kid who wasn't feeling well. I had returned as an invalid.

"I really do feel okay," I kept telling them. "I

think the medicine is kicking in. My joints don't hurt today at all."

Mom didn't seem to hear me. "Why don't you stretch out on the couch for a while?" she asked. "You've had a busy day."

What did she mean, a busy day, I wondered. I'd sat around in my hospital room, talked to the doctor and a couple of nurses, and come home in the car. How could anyone, anywhere, say I'd been busy? Nevertheless, I let Mom settle me on the living room couch and cover me with a quilt. I wasn't cold, but it would take too much energy to protest.

Energy, that's what was missing. Lying there on the couch, I felt that some vital spark had burned itself out in D-4. My body felt stronger at the moment, but I could never trust it again. I had a chronic disease. I would always be sick. Now, and next week, and next month. All summer. When I graduated from high school and started college. Every time I turned a corner in my life, the wolf would be there to greet me.

The television chattered, but I didn't try to follow the action on the screen. I closed my eyes and lay still, floating in limbo. It didn't matter where I was. The hospital, the couch at home—

it was all the same. Lupus was with me wherever I went.

When the phone rang, I didn't stir to answer it. It couldn't be for me. Why would anyone want to talk to an invalid? Eventually the ringing stopped. Then, jarring me back to the world, Caitlyn called from the other room, "Chloe, pick up, will you?"

Slowly, I sat up, letting the quilt slide to the floor, and picked up the phone from the end table. "Chloe? This is Dr. Pat! Glad you're home again!"

I remembered the last time Dr. Pat had called—back when I thought I had a stubborn strep. "Hi," I said. "It's nice to be out of the hospital, I guess."

"You guess?"

"Well—okay, it's nice." I hoped she wouldn't ask a lot of questions. I didn't want to explain about lupus.

"I've missed you over at The Shelter," she said. "Hey, remember that little brat of a beagle, the one you called Pins-and-Needles?"

I'd never be able to chase down a wild one like Pins again. I'd never have the energy for that! "Yeah," I said. "I remember her."

"She got adopted this morning! A guy came in, looked like a cowboy—boots, and a Stetson hat, like he's heading for the O.K. Corral. I thought he'd want some big, macho dog, like a malamute or something. But he took one look at Pins, and he said, 'That one!' No ifs, ands, or buts!"

"Love at first sight," I said.

"It happens," Dr. Pat said. "The amazing thing is, I got her out and handed the leash to him—and she heeled out the door like she'd been doing it all her life."

"I miss being there," I said, with a catch in my throat.

"Well, that's why I called," Dr. Pat said. "When are you coming back?"

I opened my mouth to say I'd be there on Saturday at nine o'clock, same as always. But I would never be a reliable helper again. Even if I felt well enough to go back on Saturday, how long would that last? Lupus would catch up with me sooner or later.

"I'm not coming back," I said miserably. "You'd better find someone else."

Naturally, Dr. Pat tried to make me change my mind. She said she would understand if I didn't do much of the heavy work. She still needed me in the office. If I handled the phone and the paperwork, it freed her up for other things. "I couldn't even stuff envelopes for you last time," I pointed out. "I've got to cut way back on activities. I'm supposed to get as much rest as I can."

"I really am sorry," Dr. Pat said after a while. "Give it a few more weeks before you decide for sure. I'll hold off on finding somebody new."

"That's really nice of you," I said. "But it won't make any difference. I'll still have lupus a few weeks from now."

Dr. Suarez had told us that I should "play it by ear" as far as school was concerned. "That means I should take it easy if I don't feel well," I reminded Mom as she shooed me off to bed that first night. "Maybe I'd better stay home tomorrow, just to rest up."

Mom hesitated. She looked over at Dad for help.

"She's missed almost two weeks already," he said. "What's another day, more or less?"

Wait, I wanted to protest. *Don't give in so fast! I won't break! I don't need to stay home forever, sitting on a shelf like a china doll!*

But I dreaded going back to school. I wanted

to put off the day as long as possible. If that meant playing china doll, it was fine with me.

The next day, my first full day out of the hospital, I stayed home and watched the soap operas. I was relieved to see that Francis wasn't going to leave Glenda after all, even though she'd had an affair with Raul. It was Francis she really loved. She'd only had a fling with Raul when she was jealous about Miranda. . . .

While I was in the hospital, these people in the soaps had taken on three dimensions. Now they were as real to me as Samantha or Megan McAllister. It was easy to listen in on their lives. They gave me the chance to step away from my own.

On Tuesdays Caitlyn came home at four o'clock, finished with the day's classes. From my place on the couch, I heard the front door open and the thump of her books on the hall table. Then came the voices. Caitlyn's and another—a boy's voice. With a jolt, I knew that it was Todd.

I couldn't take it in. Why was Todd Bowers here, in our house, talking to my sister? It didn't make sense. It couldn't be happening.

But I knew Todd's voice. There was no mistake. "I just thought I'd stop in and say hi," he was saying. "You know, people have been wondering."

I bet they have, I thought. I could picture the conversations over lunch: "Did you hear about Chloe Peterson? She has a disease!" "Really? What is it?" "It's a really awful one! You can't even pronounce it! She'll never get rid of it, either. She'll just have it, you know, all the time now. . . ." "Gross! You mean, like we'll be sitting at the table with somebody who's got a disease you can't even pronounce?" "Uh-huh. They say it's not catching, though." "Yeah. Sure. They *say!*" . . .

Had Todd been wondering, too? Was he asking those questions, guessing those wild guesses? Maybe he was here on a fact-finding mission, so he could go back to school with a full report.

"She's probably in the den," Caitlyn said. "Will she be surprised to see you!"

I sat up, pushing the tangled hair out of my face. My shirt was rumpled, and my pants were inches too short for me. I wouldn't even want Samantha to see me this way, let alone Todd!

Why did he keep coming back into my life? Every time he saw me, I was fainting or staggering or getting a lethal sunburn! He couldn't be interested in me, not in a boy-girl way! He felt sorry for me, that was all. He wanted to be nice.

Maybe he liked to rescue people. I gave him plenty of opportunity.

"Don't bother her if she's sleeping or something," Todd said. "Just give her these."

"Oh, that's okay," said Caitlyn. "I'll go get her."

Her steps approached down the hall, and she pushed open the door of the den. "Chloe! Guess what! Somebody's here to see you!"

"Tell him I'm asleep!" I said in a low voice.

Caitlyn stared. "Don't you want to see him? He brought you flowers!"

My heart gave a wild leap. Flowers! For me?

But no—he couldn't see me like this. If Todd had the least thought that I was still a normal girl, it would vanish if he caught a glimpse of me today.

"I can't see anybody today," I said, turning away. "Tell him I'm sleeping, please!"

"Okay," Caitlyn said, shaking her head. "No one ever said my sister was a rational being!"

"Caitlyn! Wait!" I called in a frantic whisper as she started to leave. I had to keep my voice down, so Todd wouldn't hear me. She turned back, and I pleaded, "Thank him for me, will you?"

"Okay. I'll tell him my sleeping sister says thanks a lot."

"Caitlyn! Don't pick now to be mean!"

"Oh, all right," she said, softening. "I'll tell him thank you. For the flowers. For stopping by."

"Yes," I said. "Tell him, thank you for everything."

12

thanks a lot."

"Yes," I said. "Tell him, thank you for everything."

I felt oddly conspicuous as I pushed through the
heavy front door and walked into school the
next morning. I'd been gone for so long, and so
much had changed for me! My sunburn and my
butterfly rash had disappeared, but people would
still know that I was different. How could I ever
fit in again?

"Chloe!" Samantha cried, rushing up to me
with a hug. It was an enormous relief to see her!
I laughed and hugged her back. Samantha made
me feel almost normal again. She was a shield
against some of the strangeness.

"You look great!" she exclaimed. "You don't
look like you just got out of the hospital!"

"But do you *feel* like a hospital patient?" asked

Megan, coming up beside us. "Do you feel okay now, or still sick, or what?"

Whatever she was thinking, you could count on Megan to come out with it! "I feel okay," I told her. I'd been saying that to people for months now. Sometimes the words were true, and sometimes they were not. A lot of the time I wasn't sure myself.

Sam and Megan walked me to my homeroom. Every few yards, it seemed, another wellwisher hurried over to greet me. As we approached my locker, Megan started to giggle. Sam gestured for her to be quiet, but it was too late. I knew something was up. Sure enough, when we rounded the bend in the hallway, I saw that they had decorated my locker. A red helium balloon floated overhead, anchored by a ribbon to the door handle. Streamers of crepe paper wound over the metal door from top to bottom, and magnetic letters spelled, WELCOME BACK, CHLOE!

"Oh, you guys, thank you!" I cried through a blur of tears. "You *do* make me feel welcome! You really do!"

It was wonderful to be back, I admitted to myself as I traveled from class to class through the morning. The hospital slipped quietly into the past. Bit by bit, I caught up on news and collected assignments. Joni Schubert had broken up with Bill Gambiano. Carrie Chang was after him now. Joni said she didn't care, but Megan said she sent Carrie hate-stares every chance she got. Catching up was like tuning in to the soap operas.

All morning I thought about the white carnations in the vase on the dining room table at home. Everywhere I went I kept alert for a whisper of Todd Bowers's name. What had possessed him to bring me flowers? To come to the tryout? To drop in at The Shelter on his way to buy elbow brackets? If I added all those things together, did it mean he liked me? Did I dare to hope?

As I headed for the cafeteria at the beginning of fifth period, I resolved to find Todd and thank him in person. I cruised through the room, searching table after table. When I found him at last, he was seated with Bill Gambiano and a bunch of other guys. Two timid-looking freshman girls huddled at the end. The guys paid them no attention, and they looked woefully out of place. I would look the same way, I thought, if I walked up to Todd right now. I couldn't do it. I would have to wait for a better moment.

I joined Sam and Megan at a corner table. I was digging into my salad when I realized that I had nearly forgotten my pills. I fished in my purse and brought out three little plastic containers. Two of the white ones. One yellow, and one green capsule. Conversation trailed off as I counted the pills into my palm. The others watched in silence while I swallowed them, one after another, washing each down with a swig of Coke.

"How many pills do you take, anyway?" Megan asked.

"I don't know," I said. "I've never counted. It's four times a day."

"It must be awful," Megan said. "I feel so sorry for you! We all do!"

"Well, don't," I said curtly. *Was it really true,* I wondered in dismay. *Were my friends being kind to me out of pity?* I had felt so welcome a few moments ago, as though I'd stepped back into my former place. But how could I be so sure? Would I ever know?

The talk moved on to other things. Megan lamented that her parents would ground her if she got another failure notice in Algebra Two. Sam said she'd help her study for the next test. I wondered aloud if I would ever catch up in math now. Maybe I'd have to take an incomplete for the quarter.

Suddenly I spotted Todd sauntering toward the door. He was alone. This was my chance. "Be back in a second," I exclaimed. I had no plan of action as I sprang from my seat. I simply scrambled after Todd, weaving among the tables and chairs and moving bodies until I reached him at last.

"Hey!" I called.

He stopped short, turned, and gave me a smile that made me want to dance.

"Look who's awake!" he cried. "Sleeping Beauty!"

"I'm sorry I didn't thank you last night," I began. "The flowers are great! It was so nice of you!"

"Oh, that's okay," he said. "I wanted to bring you something, but I didn't know what. My sister said flowers."

"Oh," I said dully. "Your sister."

"That sounds dumb, doesn't it?" Todd looked at the floor. Then he smiled at me again. "You're back, that's what counts," he said. "I'll walk you to study hall, okay?"

"Okay," I said. I knew I was beaming at him. It felt so good to be noticed, welcomed, admired. As I walked out of the caf with Todd Bowers, I felt that the wolf was losing ground. It trailed farther and farther behind.

Dr. Suarez sent Mrs. Smalley a note to distribute to all of my teachers. The letter explained that my attendance might be irregular. Sometimes I would need to make up tests and homework because I had systemic lupus erythematosus. Even if my teachers had never heard of my disease, the name alone was enough to intimidate them. I was glad Dr. Suarez had equipped me with that letter. Just as he predicted, my school attendance was uneven. Sometimes I began the day feeling fine, but became exhausted by third or fourth period. I'd go down to Mrs. Smalley's office and take a nap, which might last until the bell at three o'clock. Some days when I woke, I felt as though hammers were pounding inside my skull. It hurt unbearably to sit up, or even to turn over in bed. But by noon my headache would be gone, and I'd ask

Dad or Caitlyn to drive me to school for my afternoon classes. I could never plan. I could never predict how I would feel from one day to the next.

Most of my teachers were sympathetic. Graciously, they accepted the papers I turned in late, and without complaint they rescheduled the tests I missed. Mrs. Connors, my history teacher, was an extreme case. She patted my shoulder and told me in a syrupy voice that I didn't have to turn in my Civil War paper at all, if it was too much for me. I didn't like the way she spoke, as if from now on she never expected me to accomplish anything. I thanked her and said I'd write the paper. Somehow I even made the deadline.

One afternoon I went to see Mrs. Brinkerman to make up a quiz on Keats and Wordsworth. She frowned as she handed me the sheet of questions, and slammed her drawer so hard the pencils jumped on the desk blotter. It wasn't like her to be brusque with me. Dismayed, I fled to a seat in the back of the empty room. All the while I took the quiz, I felt distracted, wondering what was wrong. When I finished at last, I tiptoed to the front of the room and slipped my paper gingerly into the wire "in" basket. Mrs. Brinkerman was engrossed in a book, and I hoped I could escape without drawing her attention. But she called to me as I reached the door, jolting me to a stop.

"Chloe, wait a minute. I want to talk to you."

She had said those words to me once before. I remembered my delight when she had urged me to try out for *The Sound of Music*. But I had let her down. I'd proved she couldn't count on me. She would never ask me to try out for a play again.

I waited by the door, feeling trapped. "I'm afraid this will sound hard," she said. "But I really feel I have to say it to you."

"What is it?" I asked apprehensively.

"You're going to have to make a choice at some point," she said. "Either you'll learn to live with your illness, or you will let the illness control you."

"That's not fair!" I burst out. "I hate being sick! I do everything I can to fight it!"

"If you're not careful, lupus will end up defining you," she said.

I longed to break away, to be gone through the open door. But Mrs. B. spoke so compellingly, as if she knew something I needed to find out.

"What do you know about it?" I asked. "You haven't got lupus."

"No," she said. "But my sister—she did."

"She *had* it? You mean she doesn't have it any more?" What was she saying? Had her sister really learned to control her disease? Had she conquered it and put it behind her? Was there hope for me after all?

"She found out she had it when she was nineteen," Mrs. B. said. "That was twenty-five years ago. She passed away last August."

"She *died?*" I repeated, stunned. A chill folded around me, like a thick, clammy fog. There was no secret cure. No conquering the wolf.

"Yes," Mrs. B. said. She looked away, and I wondered if she was hiding tears. "Kidney problems," she went on at last. "That can happen with lupus—I guess you know."

"They told me. Yeah."

She straightened her shoulders and looked at me steadily. "She died at the age of forty-five," she said. "She didn't live a full life span. But that's not why I'm talking to you."

"Why *are* you, then?" I asked. My mind did

quick calculations. If I lived to be forty-five, that gave me three decades more! A lot of time! Almost endless! But what could I do with those years? How many doors remained open for me?

"The thing about Laura—my sister—was that she kind of gave up," Mrs. B. said. "The day she heard she had lupus, she gave up hope. She dropped out of college. She stopped seeing her friends. Most of the time, she just stayed home. Before she got sick, she was so much fun to be with! But she really changed. Just quit trying. Quit caring."

"How are you supposed to try," I asked, "when you're feeling rotten so much of the time?"

"If you give up, you'll feel even worse," she said logically.

"I'm getting fat, too!" I said in a rush. "I've got to take this medicine called prednisone, and it makes me all bloated!"

"There were times when Laura's lupus was under control. And even during her flare-ups, she had good days. But she was always waiting for the worst. She was afraid to go out and live."

A line of poetry popped into my head. " 'Gather ye rosebuds while ye may,' " I quoted.

" 'Old time is still a-flyin',' " Mrs. B. quoted back, breaking into a grin. We both laughed, the tension broken. I thanked her and hurried away. I was down the hall before I remembered the rest of the stanza: " 'And this same flower that smiles today,/Tomorrow will be dying.' "

13

~~~

Todd Bowers slipped into my life so gradually that he almost arrived by accident. At first, he'd stop and say hi, casually passing my table in the caf at the end of lunch period. Sometimes he rejoined his friends, but sometimes he walked me down to the Learning Center, where I usually spent my study hall.

During my second week back from the hospital, Todd began to sit down with me toward the end of lunch period. If the others were around, he threw himself into the general fun, talking and laughing with everyone. But then, when the bell rang and people scattered, he stayed with me, and we set out together through the halls.

"Are you guys an item?" Samantha asked one day. "He sure sees a lot of you lately."

"I think we're just friends," I said. "Is there such a thing as a friendship item?"

Sam shook her head. "There's only one kind," she said. "You are or you're not."

"Then it's easy," I said. "We're not."

I wished Sam would argue with me. I wanted to believe she was right. But why would Todd be interested in someone with a chronic disease? I'd even gained eleven pounds since I started taking prednisone.

But Todd did seem interested. In the third week after my return to school, he saved a place for me in the lunch line. We made our way through the line together, and after we paid for our meals, we selected a table of our own. We talked about ordinary things like TV shows and math quizzes. But all the time I felt a tingling undercurrent, like a strain of music behind our words. Of all the hundreds of girls in the room, Todd chose to sit with me. Of all the boys in the room, I wanted to sit with Todd.

"You still have that job at The Shelter?" he inquired.

It was an innocent question. He just wanted

to make conversation. But the sweet strains of music faded. Todd's words brought the wolf slinking from its lair. I could never forget lupus for long.

"I had to quit," I admitted. "I get too tired. I can't chase dogs anymore."

"Couldn't you go back when you feel better?"

"Sure, but then the next week I might be worse again. What's the point?"

"I don't know," Todd said, shifting uncomfortably. "I was just wondering."

"I miss it," I told him. "Especially I miss it on Saturday mornings, when I used to go in." I hadn't expected to say that. Somehow the words spilled out and caught me by surprise. I wished I'd kept them to myself. Boys didn't want to listen to your troubles. They liked to have fun.

As if I needed a reminder, a girl's voice broke in upon us like a sudden, crashing chord. "Hey, Todd! Whatcha doing? I never see you around these days!" Joni Schubert sauntered toward us, all long legs and shiny, swinging blond hair.

"I haven't gone anywhere," Todd said. He smiled at her, and she smiled back.

Joni draped herself over an empty chair. "I'm such a dork!" she said with a woeful giggle. "I left my wallet in the gym! Now I've got to go to Lost and Found. I'm so scared—I don't want to run into Mr. Rodriguez! He yelled at me yesterday because he said my skirt was too short!"

She might be scared of the assistant principal, but Joni overflowed with confidence when it came to boys. She was so graceful, so healthy and slim! *It wasn't fair,* I thought with a rush of fury. Why was the world full of people like Joni Schubert? They were slender and quick, while I was tired and slow and swollen from prednisone. I couldn't compete. I didn't stand a chance.

"I hate to go down there by myself," Joni hinted. "It wouldn't be so bad if I had company."

Todd glanced over at me. "Chloe and I can go with you if you want," he said.

He *did* like me, I thought joyfully. He wanted me to go along! But in the next instant my spirits collapsed. Todd was just being polite. Why would he want me trailing after him when he could be alone with Joni?

"I've got a history test tomorrow," I said. "I've got to get to the Learning Center and look stuff up on-line."

"See you, then," Todd said easily, as if it didn't

matter at all. I watched him disappear with Joni Schubert at his side.

"But he definitely likes you," Sam insisted that afternoon as we packed up our books to go home. "Can't you read the signs?"

"What do you mean?" I said. "Just because he sits at our table sometimes."

Sam banged her locker shut. "Look at the way he looks at you!" she exclaimed. "That means something!"

"What way?" I asked.

"You know," Sam said, smirking. "The Look."

"I think it's in your head," I told her as we started down the corridor. "You're making it up."

"Argue if you want to," Sam said. "I know what I know."

On the school bus, I sat by myself, listening to music on my Walkman. To ease the boredom, I opened my purse and sorted the loose change that always sank to the bottom. As I pulled out a handful of stray nickels and pennies, I came upon a crumpled comic book. I was face to face with Little Red Riding Hood and the Big Bad Wolf. Glancing furtively around to make sure no one was watching, I began to leaf through the slick pages. The booklet was designed in a question-and-answer format. Red Riding Hood asked question after question, and her kindly grandmother, in a nurse's cap and uniform, explained the wolf's behavior. "What causes lupus?" Little Red Riding Hood wanted to know. "A lot of scientists are trying to find out," her grandmother explained. "Some think lupus may be caused by a virus. Some believe that genes play an important role. Nobody knows for sure."

Why did they have to talk down to their readers like this, I thought in annoyance. *Why couldn't they treat us like grown-ups?* I was tempted to stuff the booklet into my purse and forget it again. But, somehow, I couldn't put it down. In spite of myself, I kept on reading.

Along with Little Red Riding Hood, I learned that the body normally forms antibodies, or "good guys," to attack germs and other outside invaders, "bad guys." (The antibodies were pictured as soldiers with smiley faces. The bad guys were worms with writhing antennae and dozens of creeping feet.) The various antibodies were known as the immune system. In people with lupus, the immune system was easily confused. The antibodies got so carried away that they declared war on the body's own organs. They couldn't tell that the joints and muscles, kidneys and liver belonged where they were and needed protection. The good-guy antibodies went wild and tried to destroy the body that was their own home.

As I read, I realized I had heard these basic facts before. Dr. Suarez had told us that lupus was an "autoimmune disorder," a disease in which the body seemed to turn against itself. I hadn't been able to listen that day in the conference room. It was as though my mind had shut down when I heard the words "no cure." Now I wanted to learn what I could about this disease that ruled my life. I devoured the Big Bad Wolf booklet, skipping the cute dialogue and getting to the meat on every page. I learned that lupus symptoms could increase, or flare up, at random, for unknown reasons. But some known factors could trigger a flare-up as well—stress, tiredness, certain medications, infections, and exposure to the sun. The butterfly rash that Caitlyn had hidden for me with makeup was one of lupus's distinguishing marks. Some people didn't think it looked like a butterfly at all. They said it resembled the bite of a wolf.

At the end of the booklet, Grandma gave Little Red Riding Hood a bundle of advice, packed into her empty food basket. "Eat healthy meals," I read in one package. Another contained, "Get plenty of sleep." "Find ways to relax and avoid stress." "And stay out of the sun," Grandma advised on the last page. "Make sure you always wear your hood!"

The booklet didn't suggest what Little Red Riding Hood should do if she developed a pounding headache in the middle of a test. It offered no advice if her legs felt like lead weights and she had class at the far end of the building. It didn't tell her what to do if her medications made her get pudgy, if the boy she liked turned to someone who was pretty and slim. Sorry, Grandma, I thought, tossing the comic book aside. You haven't got the answers I need.

April is not a pretty month in Illinois. Morning after morning I stepped out into a cold drizzle, the sky gray and heavy with clouds. In the old days, I used to long for spring. I hungered for bright, warm days when I could toss my coat aside, slip into sandals, and dash into the sunshine. This year, I wanted the cold to linger forever. I dreaded those first days of real, lasting spring, when people young and old would come out of hiding to drink in the sun. From now on the pleasures of sun worship belonged to other people—not to me.

"Real spring," as I once called it, burst forth on a Friday afternoon. The morning brought the cloud cover I had grown to count on. But by midday the sky cleared, and sunlight streamed through the windows. During afternoon classes, everyone was restless. Even the teachers cast yearning glances toward the world outside. It was time to be gone, time for the weekend to begin! When the final bell rang, kids stampeded for the doors, for fresh air and freedom.

I took no part in the rejoicing. Slowly, I made my way through the halls, bowed with misery. For months to come, my friends would seize every chance to lounge beside a pool or sprawl on some beach. Each gathering would be a picnic or a swim party. Within weeks, everyone I knew would sport a rich, golden tan. I alone would keep my February pallor. If I went out at all, I would slather myself with sunscreen and huddle beneath the widest umbrella, bulging out of my bathing suit. Over and over I'd hear the same question, "Why don't you get a little sun?"

How many times would I have to explain, "I have lupus. Sun exposure is bad for me."

As I passed the auditorium, I heard Mrs. Brinkerman's voice, firm and commanding: "Again. Sing your words clearly, so people can understand!" Then a song floated out to me, sweet and familiar. I stood still and remembered. "'I am sixteen, going on seventeen / I know that I'm naive . . .'"

If I didn't have lupus, I would be singing that song myself, not listening like a spy at the half-open door. If only I were rehearsing on the stage right now! I should be the one to make my words understood, to sing about being young and eager for the future! Why was I closed out of everything I wanted? Why?

Tears burned my eyes and trickled down my cheeks. I wiped the first ones away, but it did no good. Silent tears kept flowing, more and faster.

I couldn't let anyone see me like this! Fighting for control, I crouched on the floor and pretended to search through my backpack. *You've got to stop this,* I told myself. *Get up and go outside, or you'll miss the bus! Stop crying! Stop, or someone will notice!*

But already it was too late. A shadow loomed.

Someone had come to my aid. Fearfully, I looked up. Through a blur of tears, I saw Todd bending over me.

The sight of Todd's face made me cry all the harder. "Chloe," he asked, "are you okay?"

I dabbed at my eyes again. Shakily, I got to my feet. "I'm fine," I said resolutely.

"You don't look it," Todd said. "What's wrong?"

"Nothing!" I snapped. "Why do people ask that all the time?"

"I just want to know, that's all," said Todd. "You're upset, so I asked you why."

I turned away. If I opened my mouth again, I would say something terrible, something I would regret. I had to leave, to go somewhere by myself.

Todd wouldn't let me escape. "Chloe," he pleaded, "I hate to see you like this! Are you sick? Should I get somebody?"

"No!" I cried. "Quit feeling sorry for me!"

"I'm not!" he protested. "I just thought—"

"You don't understand! You never will! You're fussing over me all the time!"

"What are you talking about?" Todd exclaimed. "Fussing?"

"You know what I mean!" I rushed on. "Driving me home. Walking me to class. Asking me if I'm okay!"

"I'm trying to be nice."

"Being nice! Nice to me because I'm sick!"

"That's not it! Calm down, will you?"

"You don't know what it's like to have lupus! Nobody knows! Go see Joni, she's fine! And she's still pretty! You don't have to worry about her!"

"What?" Todd demanded. "Joni? What's Joni got to do with anything!"

I didn't bother to explain. "Leave me alone!" I shouted. "Go away and leave me alone!"

Todd looked at me, too stunned to speak. My words quivered in the silence between us. "All right, I will," he said at last. "If that's what you want." And he walked away without another word.

"Todd!" I called. "Wait! I didn't mean it! Listen!"

But he kept walking. He didn't turn his head. He didn't seem to hear me at all.

14

That night, for the first time in days, the whole family was home for dinner. It was like old times, before Dad lost his job, before Mom started to work extra hours, before I got lupus. Dad quizzed us about events in the news, and explained the latest uproar in the Middle East. Mom described the most recent computer glitch at work; the store had charged one customer twenty-four thousand dollars for three pairs of underwear. Even Caitlyn deigned to laugh over that one. Mostly she remained aloof, as though she were several levels above the rest of us. She looked a lot like Trixie and Trina, who perched regally on the windowsill as they watched the action.

Usually, I loved times like these, when we were all together, enjoying each other's company. But tonight I felt as if I were drifting on a raft, observing the people on a faraway shore. The things I'd said to Todd were out on that raft with me; they twisted around me like an entangling net. How could I treat him so badly? He had tried to be my friend—maybe even something more than a friend. And what was his reward? I hurled accusations at him, raged at him, and told him to go away.

Over and over I saw Todd's retreating back as he disappeared down the hall. I had told him to leave me alone. Now he was gone.

"You feeling all right, Chloe?" Mom asked in concern, eyeing my plate. I'd hardly taken a bite.

"I'm okay," I said. But it wasn't true this time. I had never felt so miserable in all my life.

"You're taking your pills, aren't you?" Dad wanted to know.

"Uh-huh."

"You'll let us know if anything's the matter?" Mom persisted. "You know Dr. Suarez said to pay attention to symptoms, look for patterns—"

"I'll let you know," I said dully.

"I found a couple of new sites on the Internet," Dad said. "Some doctors in Buenos Aires are treating lupus patients with bee sting."

"Bee sting!" Mom exclaimed. "Why?"

"The body reacts to bee sting with inflammation," Dad said. "It's got to do with antibodies and the immune system. That's as much as I understand."

"I'm not going to Buenos Aires to get stung," I muttered. "Forget it."

"I'm not suggesting that," Dad tried again. "Some of the stuff out there sounds rational, though. I just read where somebody's experimenting with vitamin injections. An ordinary vitamin called niacin."

He glanced at me hopefully. I should have been excited. Most of the time, I was ready to leap at any chance for restored health. But tonight, these phantom vitamin shots didn't matter.

"There's more to life than my messed-up immune system," I said, pushing my plate away.

Caitlyn came out of her feline trance. "Three cheers!" she said. "It's about time!"

"What's that supposed to mean?" I demanded. Here it was, Caitlyn sounding superior again!

"You said it yourself," she pointed out. "Lupus isn't the only thing in your life. Don't you get bored, thinking about it all the time?"

"There's nothing else *to* think about," I flashed back. "Whenever I want something, lupus gets in the way."

After the table was cleared, I went up to my room. The clutter had reached what Mom called "the point of no return." I waded through a mound of clothes, zigzagged around stacks of magazines, and sank onto my unmade bed. A phrase floated into my mind: "unrequited love." That's what you called it when you liked someone who didn't like you in return. Was there a name for what I was living through? What did they call it when you liked someone, but you convinced him that you didn't care? The language had no term for that. There wasn't any need. This didn't happen to other people. Other people didn't get themselves into this sort of mess!

How could Caitlyn dare to tell me how to deal with lupus? She wasn't the one who had this disease. She didn't know anything about it! What gave her the right to speak to me in that high-and-mighty tone of hers? Listening to her hand out advice just made me feel more alone.

If only I knew somebody else with lupus! How did other kids who had lupus deal with annoying big sisters? It would be nice to know.

Not once had I ever spoken to another person who had this illness. But I *wasn't* the only one. It would be nice to talk to someone else who knew firsthand about the aching joints, the exhaustion, and the butterfly rash. Maybe somebody somewhere had figured out how to talk to worried parents, how to control the bloating from prednisone. I had so many questions! Somewhere someone must have answers.

I hunted through the rubble on my floor for the cordless phone. It had wormed its way under the bureau, but the battery still had a charge. Perched on the edge of my bed, I punched in the number for Alice Hamilton Hospital, and asked for D-4.

My heart sank when a strange voice came on and said, "Nurses' station."

"Is the Midget—I mean—may I speak to Midge Hazeldorf?"

Usually she had the morning shift. I'd have to wait till tomorrow. But, by then, I might lose my nerve. I needed to speak with her now, this minute! Before I could change my mind.

"You want Midge?" the strange nurse asked. "Hold on a minute."

She *was* on duty tonight! I would have to talk to her! But I couldn't. I'd hang up the phone. She wouldn't know it was me who had called. I could still escape.

Escape where? If I hung up, it would be me and the wolf, alone together again.

"Hello?" the Midget's voice sounded in my ear. I could picture her there at the nurses' station, big and solid and comforting. She'd have one hand on her hip and her eyes on the hall, watching for a call light to flash on.

"Midge, it's Chloe Peterson. Remember me?"

"Chloe! How could I forget you? Hey, your warranty's not up yet—what're you calling us for?"

I took a deep breath. "Midge," I said, "have you still got room for me in your teen group? I guess I'm finally ready."

Dad drove me to Hamilton on Wednesday afternoon. He seemed delighted to be back at the hospital. He had a big smile for the lady at the front reception desk and, going up in the elevator, he greeted one of the orderlies like a long-lost buddy. You'd think he was at a college reunion, instead of the place where he had found out his daughter had an incurable disease!

It was not a joyful reunion for me. Dread gnawed at my stomach as the elevator opened and D-4 engulfed me. Instantly, I knew the smell—disinfectant and institutional food and some blend of plastic and medicine. Then came the sounds—the familiar clatter of carts and trays, the chirping of a phone at the nurses' station, the blare from an overhead speaker: "Dr. Rossi! Dr. Alfredo Rossi, call 646!" The walls were the same sickening white, in spite of the plants and cheerful pictures. I had come back to a place where I'd felt frightened and alone. This was a place where bad news descended like the blade of a guillotine to slice people's lives apart.

I relaxed a little when I spotted the Midget. She was talking to a girl in jeans and a red halter top. When she saw Dad and me, she waved us over to join them.

"Chloe!" she called. "Glad you made it! I want you to meet Latisha—she's here for Group, too."

I eyed Latisha up and down. She looked perfectly healthy. Still, something must be wrong with her, or she wouldn't be here.

Latisha studied me, too. She spoke first. "Ever been before?" she asked.

I shook my head. "What about you?"

Latisha shrugged. "I come now and then," she said. "Whenever the Midget gets on my case."

"I'm leaving you in good hands," Dad said. "I've got to go see some people downstairs. I'll meet you by the elevator in the lobby, okay?"

"Okay," I said. I wondered fleetingly which of his many Hamilton friends he would have coffee with. I wished I could go with him. I'd rather listen to Dad and his cronies talk about politics than sit through this meeting of D-4 kids.

"Go to the lounge and get settled," the Midget told Latisha and me. "The rest of the gang is there already."

At least we'd be in the lounge instead of the conference room, I consoled myself. The conference room was unbearable. I never wanted to see that painting of the ship again!

Just as I remembered, music floated through the half-open door of the lounge, sounding nothing like a hospital ward. Shouts of laughter leaped above the pounding of drums and wailing of guitars.

A bunch of kids clustered around two boys in wheelchairs, who were engrossed in a vigorous arm-wrestling match. I recognized them as Aaron and Jack, the guys I'd met the last time I visited this room.

Puffing with effort, Jack finally pushed Aaron's arm to the table between them. There was a burst of applause, and the group dispersed. "Hey, you people!" Latisha proclaimed. "It's gonna be a good day! Latisha's here!"

"Who's the new girl?" asked a boy in baggy pants.

"She's not new! She's my used-to-be roommate!" Melissa beamed at me from a seat by the window.

"Melissa!" I cried, rushing to give her a hug. I couldn't believe how happy I was to see her again.

"You're Chloe," said Jack. "I remember you." He still sounded as though he had marbles in his mouth, but somehow, today, I understood him.

"What's going to happen in here, anyway?" I asked. "Do they ask you a lot of questions?"

"What do you mean, 'they'?" said a girl in a hospital gown. The right side of her face was hidden by a massive bandage.

"It's just the Midget, all by herself," Cassie assured me. I hardly recognized her, now that she wore street clothes and was free from her IV pole.

"She asks questions, though," Aaron warned me. "She's some kind of a shrink nurse."

"A shrink nurse. That's me. I like that." The Midget strode into the room and shut the door behind her. As if on cue, the boy in the baggy pants cut the music, and we settled into a loose circle. Everyone was here for a reason. Each of us had been selected by some injury or illness. Every one of us had asked the question I had so often asked myself: "Why me?"

But the others might have problems very different from my own. Maybe none of them could tell me anything that would help. Probably I was the only person here who had lupus.

The Midget introduced me, and there came a flurry of polite, cautious greetings. "Since this is Chloe's first meeting, you guys better not try to scare her away," the Midget said, with a glint of mischief.

"*Grrrr!*" growled Howard, the baggy-pants boy, curling his hands into claws.

The Midget flung an invisible missile at his head and went on. "How's everybody's week been?"

We all looked at each other, daring someone to speak up. At last Cassie said, "I had another fight with my mom this morning."

"What about?" Aaron asked.

"The regular stuff," Cassie sighed. "She's watching me like a hawk now, every single bite I take. And then she's checking my charts and fussing that my glucose is up, and asking all the time am I okay—she drives me nuts!"

"So you told her to bug off?" asked Justina, the girl with the bandage.

Cassie giggled. "Finally, she goes, 'Let me help you with your injection, honey.' Hey, I *always* inject myself! Since when do I need her help? I lost it. Totally. I go, 'Mom, what part of *No* don't you get?'"

We all laughed. I glanced at the Midget, to see if she disapproved, but she was laughing with the rest of us. When we did settle down, though, she went into question-mode. "Why do you think your mom is so worried all of a sudden?

Like you say, she's used to you handling your diabetes yourself."

"Oh, it's because I was in here," Cassie said wearily. "She gets weird when I have a crisis."

"Sounds like my mom," Latisha put in. "She's pretty cool most of the time. But when my lupus flares up, it makes her crazy!"

My heart gave a lurch. "You have lupus, too?" I exclaimed. "Really? You do?"

"You sound like you just hit the lottery!" Latisha said. "Yeah, I've got lupus, all right. Three years now. Since I was fourteen."

"But you're thin," I blurted out. "You're not all blown up like me."

"I've been there," Latisha said, shaking her head in sympathy. "It doesn't last. When they cut down your medication, you get rid of the extra pounds."

"You don't look sick at all," I marveled. "That's what I thought as soon as I saw you."

"You look pretty okay yourself," Howard remarked, and I felt myself blush.

"That's the thing about lupus," Latisha said. "Sometimes I'm so sick I can hardly walk across the room, and nobody believes me, because I look fine."

"Same with my diabetes," Cassie put in. "Maybe it'd be easier if I had something, like a wheelchair, that shows."

Jack spoke. I only caught a few words the first time, but when he repeated the sentence, I got the gist. "You wouldn't like that, either. They talk to you like you're three years old."

I could believe it. I might have talked down to Jack myself if I didn't know him. Now I did know him, a little.

After a while, the Midget got the discussion back to parents. "How to cope with them coping with us," Howard put in.

"Me and my mom had our run-ins before I got lupus," Latisha said. "It's still the same, only now she's got a particular thing to zero in on."

"The thing that really gets my folks is when I sneak a candy bar or a couple of cookies, something that's not on my sugar-free diet," Cassie grumbled.

"Well," said Aaron, "you *did* wind up in the hospital again. Maybe they've got a point!"

"You mean, like, I should eat what I'm supposed to all the time?" Cassie looked disgusted.

"Might be worth a try," the Midget said ironically. "If you want them to quit bugging you."

Somehow the hour sped by. I didn't talk much, but I listened in fascination to the others. I learned that Jack had a head injury, the result of a car accident. Aaron had something called brittle-bone disease, that meant he'd had multiple fractures all his life. Howard had leukemia, and Justina was getting plastic surgery after a cancer operation. They spoke so casually about emergency-room visits, spinal taps, and chemotherapy, as though these experiences were normal and routine. For the first time since lupus came into my life, I was among people who might really understand.

When the meeting ended, Latisha and I went down to the lobby together. "I'm so glad I met you," I told her in the elevator. "I never knew anybody else with lupus before."

"We're some of the best people," she said grandly.

"It feels like joining a club," I said, laughing. "Admission is free."

"You don't need references, either," Latisha added. "Just wake up one day and, bingo! You're in!"

The elevator doors slid open and we staggered out, doubled up with giggles. "What'd they give you up there, laughing gas?" Dad demanded.

"Can't tell you," I gasped. "You're not a member."

"Could get to be one someday, though," Latisha assured him. "Anybody can join."

"Not anyone," I protested. "Only the best people!"

"Right!" she said, and gave me a high five. I had found a friend.

15

"Could get to be one someday, though."

On the drive home, Dad switched to the
oldies station and sang along with the Beatles. I
hadn't seen him so happy since before he'd lost
his job. Wherever he had spent the past hour,
whoever he had spent it with, he must have had
a great time.

"So, how was your rap session?" he asked as
we pulled onto the expressway.

"Dad!" I groaned. "They haven't said 'rap session' since the seventies!"

"Well, how was whatever-it-was?"

"It was pretty okay."

"You mean you liked it?" Dad asked.

"I did, really," I said. "I think I'd better keep
going for a while."

Dad cut the volume on the radio. "You want to, or you think you'd better?"

I struggled to put my feelings into words. "I didn't talk much, except to Latisha. Mostly, I listened to everybody else. But I learned a lot."

Naturally, Dad came back with the next question. "You learned what, for instance?"

"That I'm not the only one. There are lots of kids with lupus and diseases like that. Life changes when you get sick, but it doesn't stop."

I turned away and gazed out the window. I thought of all the thousands of strangers in the cars that streamed past, each one living a life I would never know. Surely, amid this vast flow of human beings on the highway, there were others who had lupus. We were coming and going with everyone else, whizzing from place to place. We were on the move, and we were unstoppable.

As I climbed the front steps, I felt a tingle of anticipation. It had been such a wonderful afternoon—surely this was a turning point. Something special awaited me at home. Perhaps I would find a message. Maybe Todd had called to say he was sorry for walking off. He would tell me that everything was all right again between us. I rushed into the kitchen and scanned the scraps of paper stuck by magnets to the refrigerator door. But no friend had called while I was out. My only message was a note to phone Dr. Pat.

My spirits sagged. Why should Todd call me? He had no apologies to make. I was the one who had told him to go away. I was the one who was sorry.

By the time I reached my room, my bright mood had faded away. The mirror on the door showed me the pounds I had gained since I started taking prednisone. I felt homely and unappealing. Would I ever return to my own face, my own natural size? Maybe I would go on expanding until I wouldn't even recognize myself.

Smooth and inviting, my bed beckoned. I threw myself facedown and closed my eyes. I was so tired. My arms and legs were like ten-pound weights, too heavy to lift. How had I ever pretended I was unstoppable? I had lupus, a disease that crushed the life out of me. What was the good of talking to those other kids in the group? All the words in the world wouldn't cure us. In the end, each of us was alone with our doubts and our pain.

Suddenly, I imagined Latisha's teasing voice inside my head. "What are you talking about, 'all alone'? You're in the club now! You're a card-carrying member!"

Only a few hours ago, I had been laughing about lupus with Latisha. We had laughed in relief because we shared this disease, with its day-to-day struggle and its endless uncertainties. Though we had just met, I knew Latisha understood this part of my life from the inside. I understood this part of *her* life, too. It was as though we had a relative in common, some nagging great-aunt who loved to drop in unexpectedly and always stayed too long.

Great-Aunt Sabina, I decided to call her. She was a glaring, sharp-chinned old lady with white hair in a tight, severe bun at the back of her neck. She was mean, she was rude, and I dreaded her visits. She could wreck my most careful plans and send me stumbling off to bed.

Latisha would love this image, I thought. We'd

giggle over our private joke all through the next meeting. We would tame the Big Bad Wolf and turn it into Great-Aunt Sabina.

If a wolf was snapping at my heels, all I could do was run in terror. But if Great-Aunt Sabina showed up, I didn't have to cower and hide. Sometimes I might even find ways to get around her. When Great-Aunt Sabina ordered me to stay home, to give up everything I cared about, I didn't have to obey her.

I sat up and swung my feet to the floor. My limbs were lighter now, ready to do as they were told. At least I could take advantage of the good times. I wouldn't let Great-Aunt Sabina snatch those away from me.

This time the cordless phone was on my CD shelf. When I pulled it out, a tier of plastic boxes cascaded to the carpet. I'd get to them later. Right now I had a purpose. I punched in Dr. Pat's number and waited.

"Dr. Pat," I said when I heard her voice on the other end. "This is Chloe. You left me a message."

"Yes," she said. "I just wanted to touch base with you. I wondered how you're feeling."

"Okay for the moment," I said. "I was even

wondering"—I drew a deep breath—"I was wondering if I can come back to work."

"Aha!" Dr. Pat exclaimed. "Great minds follow the same channels!"

"You mean I can? It's okay with you?"

"That's why I called today."

I hesitated. "I don't know if I can do a lot of chasing and lifting and stuff. I don't think I could catch a wild pup like Pins if I'm having a bad day."

"You'll do what you can," Dr. Pat said. "There's a troop of Brownies coming to visit on Saturday. I could use some help showing them around."

I still felt a need to forewarn her. "I might be sick sometimes. I might not be able to come in every week. I'd hate to let you down."

"We'll work around it," she promised. "One nice thing about The Shelter, we can be flexible."

"You want me to come this Saturday?" I asked.

"Can you make it?"

"If everything goes okay, I'll plan to be there."

After I put down the phone, I sat for a long moment. For better or for worse, I had made a choice. Lupus wouldn't allow me to gallop through life, bounding inexhaustibly from one activity to another. I had to select carefully, budget my limited energy. Maybe I'd never star in another musical; maybe I'd never have the stamina for those long rehearsals, night after night. But it was within reason to believe I could handle my Saturday job. I missed my work at The Shelter, and Dr. Pat wanted me back. Somehow we would iron out whatever bumps came along.

That very night, as I was upstairs coming to terms with Great-Aunt Sabina, Dad was on the Internet, learning about the lupus cure.

He didn't tell me the news right away. He told Mom first, and they talked it over late into the night. Mom wasn't sure they should say a word to me until they had spoken with Dr. Suarez. But Dad persuaded her that I had a right to know. It was my future they were talking about. It was my life.

Normally, I got up at quarter to seven on school days. The next morning, Mom knocked on my door at six. "Come down to the kitchen," she said. "We need to talk to you before I leave for work."

Grumbling and disgruntled, I threw on a bathrobe and padded downstairs in my furry slippers. Dad and Mom awaited me at the breakfast table. They looked so serious, I thought—with a pang of fear—that someone must have died.

"There's a team of doctors doing some interesting work out in Denver," Dad said, paging through a sheaf of papers beside his plate. "Their article says they may have the answer." He didn't have to tell me which answer he meant.

I looked from Dad to Mom, studying their faces for clues. This wasn't about bee stings or boiled herbs. This article was special, something to build our hopes on. Then why didn't Mom and Dad swoop me up and dance me around the kitchen? Why weren't they overjoyed?

"What do they say?" I asked. "What do I have to do?"

"You don't *have* to do anything," Mom said hastily. "It's still in the experimental stage."

"*What* is?" I asked. The way they looked, this wasn't going to be simple.

"It's a complete bone-marrow transplant," Dad said. "The blood cells are manufactured by the marrow, and blood cells contain your immune cells. So, if you've got all new bone marrow, you can get a whole new *healthy* immune system."

"You mean I'll be cured?" I exclaimed. "No more lupus?"

"If it works, you'd be cured," Dad said.

Before I could jump out of my chair, Mom repeated, "*If* it works."

"First thing, they have to find a donor who's a proper match for you," Dad began.

"Is that all?" I cried. "Hey, they have this nationwide database. I saw it on 60 *Minutes*. They can find someone to match me."

"That's the *least* of our problems," Mom said grimly. "The hard part is, before they give you the transplant, they've got to kill off all the marrow in your own body."

"You mean they drill into my chest with a giant needle?" I asked with a shudder, remembering Melissa.

"I don't know about that part," Mom said. "They have to give you chemotherapy, these very powerful drugs, to kill all the marrow cells you have."

I couldn't rein in my excitement any longer. "Let's go!" I said eagerly. "Let's take a trip to Denver!"

"Wait!" Mom held up a restraining hand. "We need to think about this. These drugs are very strong. They'll make you feel sick—unbelievably sick—for three weeks." She paused before she went on. "We called Dr. Suarez last night and asked him about all this. He says there's a 'significant risk.'"

"Risk of what?" I asked.

Dad spoke slowly, wearily. "There's a ten percent chance that you wouldn't survive."

Ten percent . . . survive. The words swam before my eyes. What was ten percent? Ten people out of a hundred. Ten would die, and ninety would live, maybe even be cured of lupus forever.

"Dr. Suarez thinks it's too soon," Mom said. "There's only been one study so far. We need to know a lot more."

"But did he agree I could be cured?" I asked. "Does he say it *could* happen?"

"It seems to work for some people," Dad said.

"Not for those ten percent," said Mom. "It sure didn't work for them."

Dad turned to me. "You're the one who really knows what it's like to have lupus," he said. "You need to weigh everything, and tell us how you feel about all this."

I stared down at my bowl of Rice Krispies. I

had no interest in food. "I'll be thinking," I said. "I don't know how I can think about anything else."

I remembered that terrible day back at Hamilton, when I cried to the Midget, "If I have to have lupus for the rest of my life, I'd rather die!" Now I would be put to the test.

16

The dogs barked a frantic greeting as I walked into The Shelter that Saturday morning. I hadn't been there in nearly three months. Most of my old friends had been adopted, to be replaced by a lively crop of new arrivals. The dogs didn't remember me, but their joyful yips and woofs, their leaping and wagging, made me feel utterly welcome.

So did Dr. Pat. "I sure am glad to see you!" she exclaimed, beaming. "We've got seventeen Brownies coming in twenty minutes."

As we spoke, a big black dog emerged from beneath the desk. Mike walked toward me, head high, tail waving. He sniffed my outstretched hand, and I rubbed his sleek head. "He's such a sweet old guy," Dr. Pat said. "I decided he's a keeper."

"Kind of an office mascot!" I said in delight. "A cage was really beneath his dignity."

"I hear you may take a trip pretty soon," Dr. Pat remarked. "Denver's a great town."

"Mom told you?"

She nodded. "Anything new on it?"

"Dr. Suarez isn't crazy about the idea, but he's helping us check it out. They drew a couple bottles of my blood for tests, to see if I'm a good candidate."

"Sounds like you're running for president," she said.

"That's what it feels like," I agreed. "If I get in, they've got to find me the right bone-marrow donor. They'll test Mom and Dad and Caitlyn first, since they're my closest relatives."

"And you really want to go ahead with this?"

I scratched Mike's head, and he leaned against my legs with an expression of sheer bliss. "I don't know," I admitted. "Sometimes yes, and sometimes I'm totally scared. I just don't know at all."

The Brownies swarmed in right on schedule, and I led them on a grand tour. They chattered and giggled and fawned over Mike. They wanted to pet all the puppies and kittens. A little girl named Isabel fell in love with a half-grown tiger cat, and announced she'd be back with her mom to take him home.

I thought of Todd as I showed the girls around. Once upon a time, I had given him the same grand tour. In those long-ago days, he sought me out. He wanted to know about my life. Maybe we would have become an "item," as Samantha would say. I had been so absorbed in my illness and my fears that I never gave him a real chance. Now it was too late. He'd turn to Joni Schubert. She wouldn't be any trouble. She didn't have lupus.

The girls thanked us profusely and gave us a poster they had made, announcing KITTENS AND PUPPIES FOR FREE. Their giggles faded as they trailed after their leader across the parking lot. I sank into a chair for a rest. Because of lupus, I had to take a break. I couldn't rush from here to there, juggling three activities at once, as I had in the old days. And lupus made me impatient and short-tempered with the people around me. Because of lupus, I had lost Todd Bowers.

Thinking about Todd filled me with certainty. If I could get into the transplant program, I'd be on the next plane. I'd risk anything for the chance to be rid of this disease that was ruining my life.

When I reached home, I found two messages on the refrigerator door. The first was from Samantha, asking me to go shopping tomorrow with her and Megan. That would work. I could take it easy for the rest of today, and tomorrow I'd have the energy to walk the malls.

The second message was from Dr. Suarez. Caitlyn had jotted it down at ten-forty-five that morning. It simply said, "Will call back."

My heart gave a wild lurch. What did it mean? Had I been accepted into the program already? Or was I ruled out as a possible candidate?

Calm down, I warned myself. The message might mean he had to draw yet another vial of blood. It could mean anything. It might mean nothing at all.

Gazing around the familiar kitchen, breathing in the faint fragrance of Mom's spices, I was suddenly very glad to be alive. Not even Great-Aunt Sabina could steal away the pleasures of everyday living. I had my family, my home, my friends. Dr. Pat needed me, and Trixie and Trina purred at my feet. I still had so much to live for, in spite of lupus.

I called Samantha and told her I'd meet her tomorrow. "Two o'clock, in front of the Jewel Supermarket," she said. "You know—where the sign is."

"I know," I said, a little impatiently. "How many times have we met there?"

"Just be sure you make it," Samantha said. "Don't be late or anything."

"Two o'clock. I heard you the first time."

"Just want to make sure," she said. "See you then. In front of the Jewel."

"You made your point," I said. "I'll be there!"

Mom came in as I hung up the phone. She wore a shining smile and carried a big, square box from the bakery. "A cake?" I inquired. "How come?"

"To celebrate!" she said, setting it gently on the counter.

"Celebrate what?"

Mom shook her head. "It's a surprise," she said. "Let your dad tell you tonight."

While I was out, Dr. Suarez must have talked to Dad. I had been accepted. They wanted to tell me the good news when the whole family was together. We would celebrate. It would be like a birthday, the beginning of my new, healthy life.

Mom was radiant. She bustled around the kitchen, rattling through the cupboards, making ready for a feast. But she was the one who didn't trust the bone-marrow program. She wanted to wait for months, or even years, until the experiments were finished. It was Mom who kept reminding us about the "ten-percent mortality rate." If I were accepted, would she really find cause for celebration?

Something told me not to ask. Mom said Dad wanted to tell me himself. I would have to wait. Somehow.

There were moments when I yearned to lap up the sunshine with every pore. This was one of those times. Almost unbearably, I needed to be out of the house, to feel fresh air on my skin, to be renewed by the spring weather. I was allowed only the glassed-in sundeck, where the windows screened out the ultraviolet rays that were so dangerous to me. I tilted back in Dad's lounge chair and watched the trees swaying in the light breeze. Through the lacework of leafy branches, cars glided by, their sound muffled by the double panes. I saw our neighbor, Mr. Patterson, come home with a load of groceries. Mrs. Moranti across the street arrived with a carload of kids. If I had the bone-marrow treatment, if it proved successful, I'd be out there to greet the neighbors. I'd wave and call from my chair on the lawn, just another kid trying to catch some rays.

If the treatment worked, I'd go to every pool party all summer long. I'd be one of the gang again, a normal kid with a normal summer tan.

If only, I thought with a burst of longing. *If only* . . .

Just before suppertime, Dad walked in with a dozen long-stemmed roses. "In honor of the occasion," he said, handing them to Mom and giving her a kiss. The way they grinned at each other, I could almost forget they were grown-ups.

I looked at Dad expectantly. When would he tell me the news? Was I leaving for Denver next week? What was going on? Why didn't anyone tell me?

Even Caitlyn was curious. She sidled into the kitchen as Mom put the roses in water, and asked in her bored, languid way, "What's going on?"

"The waiting is over!" Dad proclaimed. "I got the final word today! I have a job!"

In the first instant, I felt a pang of disappointment. All this excitement had nothing to do with a call from Dr. Suarez. It wasn't about me at all. Then relief swept in like a warm, healing tide. Dad's search for work was over at last! The tension was at an end. Family life would fall into a comfortable pattern once again. We would all be happier now, and more secure.

"Where will you be working?" I asked.

"You won't believe this," Dad said. "I'll be Director of Public Education and Outreach at Alice Hamilton Hospital."

"You're kidding!" I exclaimed. "You're going to work at Hamilton? Doing what?"

"They have a lot of programs to teach people about health issues," Dad explained. "Screenings for certain diseases, preventive info about things like lead paint. They go out to schools and organizations, things like that. Well, that's the department I'll be directing."

"You always did like that place," I said, laughing. "Way more than I do."

"I interviewed when you went to your group last week," Dad said. "They just let me know their final decision."

We had a festive supper that night. Mom spread a tablecloth, and Caitlyn hunted up cloth napkins with lace trim. I even found a pair of brass candlesticks, and lit a candle at each end of the dining room table. I tried to imagine my own father working at Hamilton. Maybe I'd run into him when I went in for appointments. He might meet Jack and Aaron and Cassie and the rest of the kids in my group. He'd greet them in the halls like old friends, and I'd squirm with embarrassment. *Oh, well*, I told myself. I could adjust. I could adjust to almost anything.

The phone rang just as Mom was cutting the cake. Dad picked it up, and the room fell silent. "Yes," he said. "We got your message. Thanks. . . . She is? She's on the waiting list? That's wonderful. I'll tell her. Thank you from all of us."

"The waiting list?" I repeated when he hung up the phone. "What does that mean? Am I accepted or not?"

"You're through the first level," Dad said. "It means that when your name comes up on the waiting list, they'll do more tests and decide if you can try the transplant treatment."

"How soon?" Mom asked.

"It could be this summer," Dad said. "Of course, we can always say no. We don't have to go through with this."

"It's only a waiting list," Mom said. "Right?"

Caitlyn passed me a slice of cake. "What do you think?" she asked. "You still want to go for it?"

"I don't know," I sighed. "I really don't know."

To be on the safe side, I had Mom drop me off in front of the Jewel at one-forty-five. Sam had been in a real snit about my being on time. Maybe she thought I was turning into another Megan McAllister.

I found a shady spot at the edge of the parking lot, a stone's throw from the sign, and waited. The minutes ticked slowly by as cars pulled out and in, shopping carts clanged, and Sam failed to appear. I'd have fun teasing her if she showed up late herself!

I was on the lookout for the green van Sam's mother usually drove. When a dark-blue Chevy pulled up, I barely gave it a second glance. Then the door slammed, and a tall figure came forward. I took a second look. My heart began to race. It couldn't be Todd. It couldn't be! Yet, somehow, unbelievably, here he was, stepping toward me across the pavement.

"Chloe?" he said, his voice careful.

"Todd." I couldn't think of anything more to say, just that clear statement of his name.

"Hi," he said. "How's it going?"

"What are you doing here?" I gasped.

"Nothing much. I just thought I might run into you. And—you know—I want to talk to you."

How did he know I'd be in the Jewel parking lot on this Sunday afternoon? I could make no sense of the puzzle. But, at last, I took in the rest of his words, the part that mattered. "You want to talk to me? Why?"

"I was hoping maybe we could—you know—clear things up."

He waited, watching me closely. I was the one who had gotten angry. I had told Todd to go away. I had hurt him. It was up to me to set things right between us.

I drew a deep breath. "Listen," I said, "I don't know what got into me that day at school. I just kind of lost it. It was really stupid of me."

Todd didn't say anything. I knew I had to go still further. "You were trying to be nice, and I got mad," I faltered. "I wish it hadn't ever happened."

I struggled for air. This dizziness had nothing to do with lupus. At last I found the words I needed. "Todd," I breathed, "I'm sorry."

"It's okay," he said. "It's okay." In an instant, he crossed the last distance between us and took me in his arms. I felt myself melt against him. His hand brushed my hair and tilted my face up to meet his in a soft, sweet kiss.

"I guess I make a lot of mistakes," Todd said, gently letting me go. "I want to try and do better, all right?"

"I get too upset sometimes," I said. "Things get me down, and I blame other people. That's not right."

"It's dumb to fight," Todd said. "I mean, we could do something fun instead. Like go to a movie."

"What?" I asked, dazed.

"A movie. You know. We could even go this afternoon. There's one that starts at two-forty."

"Wait," I stammered. "I can't. I'm meeting Sam. She'll be here any second."

Todd laughed. "Sam's at her aunt's house," he said. "She's not coming."

I stared at him blankly. "You talked to her? She told you?"

"Sure, I talked to her! We worked it all out!"

Finally the truth began to dawn. "You mean,

you and Sam set this up?" I asked. "You got her to trick me into coming here today?"

"Something like that."

"You did all that, just to see me? That's not fair!" I cried, and I was laughing, too.

"All's fair in love and war," Todd said. He was grinning, as if it were a big joke. But I'd heard that word. *Love*. He couldn't take it back.

"You really want to see a movie?" I asked him.

"Sure. Can you?"

"Looks that way," I said. "Looks like all of a sudden I've had a change of plans."

17

~~~

The school year was almost finished by the time I made it to another meeting of the teen group at Hamilton. By then, Dad was installed in his new job, and he proudly showed me around his office. He had a big mahogany desk, a padded swivel chair, a wall of bookcases, and—to his disappointment—a view of the parking lot. But the sign on the door said: PROGRAM DIRECTOR. While I was there, the phone rang three times. I got the feeling that my dad was doing important things at Hamilton Hospital.

Latisha greeted me when I stepped off the elevator onto D-4. "Hey!" she said, slapping my palm in a high five. "You look great!"

"Nice try," I said. "I've put on twenty-three pounds now. It's disgusting!"

"As soon as they cut down your prednisone, it'll start to come off," she assured me. "It comes off as fast as it piles on."

"That's what Dr. Suarez tells me," I said. "I've got to get used to this up-and-down stuff somehow."

"Somehow, you do," Latisha said, sighing. "It's part of being in our club."

"The good part is, I feel better than I have in months," I told her as we headed into the lounge. "Dr. Suarez says my symptoms are getting under control."

"Hope it lasts," Latisha said, shaking her head. "One time I was perfect for eight months."

"And then it came back?"

"Oh, yeah," she laughed. "You know Great-Aunt Sabina—she never stays away for good."

The group was never the same twice in a row. I was glad to see Cassie and Melissa back, but Aaron and Jack were missing today. A new boy named Josh said he was waiting for a kidney transplant. He told us his older sister was the best tissue match. "We never got along that good," he said wryly. "I was scared she'd say 'No way, José! I ain't letting them cut me up for that twerp!' But she's being really cool about it. Really cool."

How would it feel to wonder if your own sister might refuse to help you survive? It was impossible to imagine. Every one of us was struggling with something, I thought. Josh and Cassie and the others all lived with illness, just as I did. We each tried to make the best of what we had. We fought to live as fully as we could. To live, that was what counted. Not just to eat and breathe, but really to live a life that meant something.

The last time I had come to the group, I didn't talk much. But today, as I listened to Josh, I knew I had something to say. "I'm on the waiting list for a transplant, too," I began. "A bone-marrow transplant. I'm not sure who would give me the marrow, but—" I hesitated. "It doesn't matter, at this point."

"What do you mean?" Cassie asked. "I'd want to know if I were you."

"I would, too, if I was going to actually get this treatment," I assured her. "The thing is, it's experimental. They're not even sure it'll work. And, right now, it's dangerous."

"Like, how dangerous?" Melissa asked.

"Like, you could die," I said. "One chance out of ten."

No one spoke. I felt their eyes upon me, taking me in, trying to understand the decision I faced. I felt their caring as they waited for me to say more.

"Right now, I feel pretty well. It's hard to believe I'll ever be sick again," I went on. "But with lupus, it could change overnight. Tomorrow I might be too weak to get out of bed."

"You got that one right," Latisha agreed.

"There's a chance this treatment could cure me," I said. "I'd never have lupus again. But there's a chance it could kill me, too."

Latisha bent forward, listening intently. I wondered if her doctor knew about Denver. Sometime soon it might be Latisha's turn to make this same choice.

"What do your parents think?" Josh asked.

"Mom is totally against it. So is Dr. Suarez—he thinks it's too early to try, the data's not in yet. Dad says we should find out as much as we can and then make up our minds."

"That can't hurt," Latisha said. "Finding out won't kill you."

"I've been going back and forth, back and

forth," I said. "But, sitting here this afternoon, I realize I've made up my mind. I really *do* know."

"So, what'd you decide?" asked Melissa.

I drew a deep breath. It was going to be hard to say these words aloud.

"Remember, Melissa, when we were roommates back in March? Remember what I said one time?"

Melissa nodded. She had never forgotten. Surely the Midget remembered, too. But I had to tell the others. "I said I'd rather die than live with lupus," I admitted. Tears stung my eyes, and I added, "Now I feel ashamed that I said that. I was so mad and upset, I thought I meant it."

"You didn't?" the Midget asked gently.

"I did in that moment," I said. "I felt like lupus was winning. I was torn apart by it."

I paused, hoping the right words would come. I thought of Mrs. Brinkerman and her sister, the one who had spent twenty-six years at home, waiting for the worst. "I don't want to die," I said simply. "I want to live my life."

"Then you don't want to go for that bone-marrow treatment?" Latisha asked.

"Not yet," I said. "It's too chancy. I can live with lupus if I have to. It's a lot better than being dead."

When the group disbanded, I was supposed to meet Dad for a ride home. But I didn't go down to his office right away. I walked the length of the corridor, and remembered how I had paced up and down in those first despairing days after my diagnosis. I had been so frightened then, and so alone.

When I reached the end of the hall, I stood and gazed through the tall window hung with plants. From here, the view was magical. The sun glinted on the lake, and the wind churned whitecaps along the shore. Off in the distance, a sailboat skimmed the water, quick and graceful as a bird in flight. I watched it until it disappeared. Then I went back to the elevator and pressed the "Down" button. It was time for me to go.

When the group disbanded, I was supposed to meet Dad for a ride home. But I didn't go down to his office right away. I walked the length of the corridor, and remembered how I had paced up and down in those first despairing days after my diagnosis. I had been so frightened then, and so alone.

When I reached the end of the hall, I stood and gazed through the tall window hung with plants. From here, the view was magical. The sun glinted on the lake, and the wind churned whitecaps along the shore. Off in the distance, a sailboat skimmed the water, quick and graceful as a bird in flight. I watched it until it disappeared. Then I went back to the elevator and pressed the "Down" button. It was time for me to go.

About the Author

Deborah Kent grew up in Little Falls, New Jersey, where she was the first totally blind student to attend the local public school. She received her B.A. in English from Oberlin College, and earned a master's degree from Smith College School for Social Work. She worked for four years in community mental health at the University Settlement House on New York's Lower East Side.

In 1975 Ms. Kent decided to pursue her lifelong dream of becoming a writer. She moved to the town of San Miguel de Allende, Mexico, which had an active colony of writers and artists. In San Miguel she wrote her first young-adult novel, *Belonging*. She also met her future husband, children's author R. Conrad (Dick) Stein.

Deborah Kent has published more than a dozen novels for young adults, as well as numerous nonfiction titles for middle-grade readers. She lives in Chicago with her husband and their daughter, Janna.